Praise for *Stranded in Boringsville*

"This entertaining story will hook readers with the engaging characters and their experiences. Its tone is refreshing and genuine."

—VOYA

"Enjoyable and quirky."

—School Library Journal

"Giving people—and places—a closer look is the exceptionally handled theme. . . . Twelve-year-old Rain's narration alternates with smart, chess-playing Daniel's, whose entries take the form of *Star Trek* captain's logs. . . . Both protagonists provide humorous, lively narratives filled with creative descriptions."

—The Horn Book

"Bateson deftly allows Rain and Daniel to chronicle their budding friendship and the problems each has fitting in at home and at school. . . . Readers will ache for the kids, whose conflicted feelings seem all too real."

—Booklist

"A fresh, lively, and readable exploration of a situation with which many readers will identify."

—The Bulletin

Stranded in Boringsville

Catherine Bateson

Holiday House / New York

© Catherine Bateson
First published 2002 by University of Queensland Press,
Box 6042, St. Lucia, Queensland 4067 Australia
under the title Rain May and Captain Daniel
First published in the United States of America
by Holiday House, Inc. in 2005
All Rights Reserved
Printed in the United States of America
www.holidayhouse.com
3 5 7 9 10 8 6 4 2

Library of Congress Cataloging-in-Publication Data
Bateson, Catherine, 1960–
Stranded in boringsville / by Catherine Bateson.
p. cm.
Originally published : Australia: University of Queensland Press, 2002.
Summary: Following her parents' separation, twelve-year-old
Rain moves with her mother to the country, where she befriends
the unpopular boy who lives next door and also seeks a way
to cope with her feelings toward her father and his new girlfriend.
ISBN 0-8234-1969-X (hardcover)
[1. Moving, Household—Fiction. 2. Divorce—Fiction.
3. Interpersonal relations—Fiction. 4. Conduct of life—Fiction.
5. Australia—Fiction.] I. Title.
PZ7.B3222St 2005
[Fic]—dc22
2004060739
ISBN-13: 978-0-8234-1969-2 (hardcover)
ISBN-10: 0-8234-1969-X (hardcover)
ISBN-13: 978-0-8234-2113-8 (paperback)
ISBN-10: 0-8234-2113-9 (paperback)

For Anna, Sasha and Helen
who all became country girls
and with thanks to Alasdair,
resident Trekkie.

Moving to Boringsville

When Dad moved out of our home and into Julia's apartment, Mum changed her name to Maggie, put our house up for sale and had a huge clean-out. I didn't mind the first and last things so much, but I hated the idea of selling our house.

'We have to sell, chickadee,' Mum said. 'It's the settlement arrangement your father and I made. Anyway, I don't want to live here. We need a fresh start. We're going to live in Granny's old house.'

'But that's in the country. We can't move to the country.'

'It's perfect timing, really — the tenant who was there has handed in his notice. He's moving to Tasmania for the landscapes,' Mum said as though she hadn't heard me.

'I don't understand. Why?'

'He's an artist. Apparently he wants to paint in Tasmania.'

'No Mum, Maggie — I mean, why do we have to move? What about school? What about my friends?'

'You'll have a new school.'

'But it's halfway through the year. I can't change now.'

'You'll have to,' Mum said. 'I'm sorry, Rain, but that's all there is to it.'

'I won't know anyone. And the country! Boringsville.'

'Well, that's exactly one of the reasons I think we should move,' Maggie said. 'The country is the only place one can stand still for long enough to hear your own heartbeat. I'm sick of this rushing. I rush in the morning to get everything ready to begin a day of rushing. I rush home in the evening to get to bed early enough to start all over again the next day. And what have we to show for it? A bookshelf full of self-help books on achieving a stress-free life and a credit card debt. It's time for a new life, Rain.'

I hoped the house wouldn't sell. I refused to clean up my bedroom, and when the agent showed people through, I made sure that the rug in the lounge room was askew so they could see the burn in the carpet underneath and I complained loudly about the water pressure, the neighbours' cats and the traffic noise. No one paid any attention. People commented instead on all the things I loved about the house — the ceiling rose in the lounge room, the neat kitchen with its breakfast nook, the fig tree in the backyard.

After people had walked through our house and touched the walls and paced out the size of the rooms, Maggie and I would walk up to the shops and buy fish and chips and eat them in front of the television without saying anything.

The house was sold to a couple. He wore a pin-stripe suit and she wore bright lipstick and I hated them because they sighed when they saw the concrete backyard and rolled their eyes at the old stove in the kitchen and tutted about the toilet being in the bathroom rather than separate. Maggie didn't care.

'It's their house now,' she said, 'or will be on settlement date. And we'll be starting a new life, Rain, in a new house.'

'An old one,' I pointed out, 'and run down. You said so yourself.'

I like having the last word.

As soon as the contract was signed, Mum started the Big Clean Out.

'I'm simplifying my life,' she said, flinging clothes into op shop bags, emptying drawers and stacking box after box of paper for recycling. 'No more stuff for the sake of it. Everything must be useful or beautiful.'

She threw out things I didn't know we had, like an old black and white television set, some zoo-print curtains — unfinished — a whole lot of old vinyl records and a tennis trophy my father had overlooked in his move. I watched as she piled it all in the back of the car for the op shop and I knew I should have rescued the tennis trophy and given it to Dad next time I saw him, but I didn't. I just watched it go off to the op shop with the rest of the junk.

Maggie was all glittery and brittle the day of the move. She spoke to the removalists in a thin voice that tried to be jolly. She asked them things about schools in the area, what the weather was like now, the state of rural health funding and how they liked living in Clarkson.

The young guy just mumbled into his Blundstones, but his father grunted out replies while he heaved our boxes and wardrobes.

'School's good,' he said, 'small — about sixty odd. My three went there. When Jeff went through there weren't even sixty, were there? Bloody cold, but. What's your heating like?'

'Wood fire,' Maggie said. 'I suppose it still works. I honestly haven't seen the place for a few years — not since we cleared it out after my mother died. We've had tenants in it.'

'Yes — that artist bloke. He kept it quite well — did a bit of gardening. You'll have to get someone in to check your chimney flues, make sure they're all right. Order some wood in — I don't think he will have left you any — didn't seem to do much cooking. Ate at the pub most nights.'

'Is there someone local to look at the flues?' Maggie sounded less jolly.

'Oh sure. I'll give Mick a hoy, he'll do it for you. Get him on the phone, Jeff, tell him to check out the flues in the old Carr place and drop round some wood at the same time.'

Jeff mumbled and ducked out to the truck.

'You needn't worry about rural health.' Jeff's dad laughed. 'You're living right next to the doctor.'

'Oh, that's useful,' Maggie said in an undecided way.

After the removalist left, Fran, Mum's best friend, came over and helped us say goodbye to the house. I went through room by room promising them I would never forget them. Mum and Fran hugged a lot, then Fran cried and Mum put on her sunglasses and we drove off. Just drove off.

'Don't look back,' Mum said. But I did and I saw Fran waving her hankie as though we were going on a long, long journey.

'The great thing about starting afresh,' Maggie said, putting her foot on the accelerator to emphasise her words, 'is that you get this wonderful chance to reinvent yourself, to become the person you want to be. Who do you want to be, Rain? It's your choice, darling — anyone in the world.'

I thought about it. Seriously, what I would like to do is to dye my hair a far-out galaxy blue, pierce my ears five times, right up to their pixie tips, and wear a lot of black, or purple, or orange. I'd like to be positively brilliant at one thing — designing houses or painting pictures or writing science fiction stories. And I'd like to have a wild bedroom with a dark blue ceiling and the whole of the milky way painted on it in glow-in-the-dark paint. I'd like to be a little mysterious and have my whole grade talking about me, half-scared of my cleverness and sarcasm, but I'd also like one special friend. We'd swear eternal love and when we had daughters we'd call them after each other so they'd grow up special friends, too.

Maggie wanted to practise serenity and harmony. She was giving up executive stress and office politics. She didn't even want to be on the School Council. She wanted to meditate for an hour a day, do yoga and rediscover her creative self. She wanted to find herself a place in a small community. She wanted to chill out for a couple of years, grow vegetables and plant her feet firmly on the earth.

'I'll leave the stress and office politics to your father and Julia,' she said. 'They can worry about money and investments and getting to the top of the food chain. I'm sick of it. I want a real life you can measure by heartbeats, not in debit and credit columns.'

I didn't understand quite what she was talking

about. If she meant my father had been obsessed by money, she was wrong. He might be obsessed by work, I'd give her that — but not money. Dad hands out money like it's tissues and never asks for the change back.

I didn't want her to get on to what went wrong between her and Dad, so I started humming something which could have been a song from the Acid Indigo or might, on the other hand, have been from Circus Ponies. I wasn't quite sure myself, but it was nice and loud and made my lips and the inside of my nose tingle.

'Well,' Maggie said, getting the hint after a minute of humming, 'well, won't it be fabulous settling all our stuff in a new house. And think of the backyard, Rain — it's such a beautiful space for a child. We'll be able to plan a really wonderful garden there with secret places and little meditation spots and it will be quite magical. I always felt terribly sorry for you in that poky narrow Brunswick garden.'

Actually I loved our Brunswick garden. Yes, most of it was concrete, but that was great for rollerblading and scootering. I loved the cherry tomatoes Mum had planted in my old plastic swimming pool and, even though you couldn't climb it, I loved the big fig tree out the back. In fact, the more I thought about it, the more our old backyard had going for it: the rosemary bush, for example, the leaves of which were delicious with roast potatoes and lamb, and the grape-vine which regularly produced bunches of grapes each summer. It hurt me that someone else was going to enjoy such bounty every year.

'Granny's garden is twice as big,' Maggie interrupted as though she had read my mind, 'so there's twice as much space to do things. And don't you remember the wonderful apples we'd harvest from her trees when you were little? And the damson plums, too — every year, branches drooping to the ground heavy with fruit. Mum would make jam, damson cheese and plum sauce.'

I remembered Granny quite well. Her face was all soft, like flower petals. I remembered stroking it when she had a headache. And sleeping with her in her bed when Mum and I would visit and how she would smell musty, like op shops and old books. I'd wake her up in the morning and she'd have to put her false teeth in before she went out to make breakfast but she'd talk to me without them and her words would be all blurred. She would tell me stories about when she was a little girl. She was chased through a paddock by a bull once and only escaped because her cousin Harry hauled her through a gap in the fence by her frilly knickers.

'I miss her,' Maggie said. 'I miss knowing she's up here. I think that's when it all started with your father and me, after Mother died. People dying, your mother dying, makes you think about how *you* are living.'

I could see how Maggie would miss Granny and I thought I did too, a bit. It's funny — I don't miss Dad the way I thought I would. I thought I'd miss him all the time. Instead I've become used to talking to him on the phone. And then sometimes I miss him so sharply it's like an ice-cream headache, the sort you get when you eat really cold ice-cream on a hot day. I miss hearing him come home after work and I miss hearing them talking at night. I miss Sunday mornings when he would cook great big breakfasts of pancakes, bacon or banana fritters. Now, when I'm over at his new place, we go out for breakfast. Julia likes to do that. She's latte dependent, she says. The juice is always good but you never get quite enough bacon, I reckon. And it's a bit dippy, sitting out where everyone can see you having breakfast.

'Coming into Clarkson,' Mum said, interrupting my thoughts, 'weather crisp, no air turbulence. Oh, look, they've got a new Welcome to Clarkson sign up.'

'Wineries,' I read on the big green sign, 'craft, galleries. Gosh, it doesn't look as though there's room for all that.'

'Darling, there's the school.'

It was just a school. I refused to be impressed.

'Cruising down the main drag of Clarkson,' Maggie said.

'Right Mum, there's a newsagency, a baker — watch that dog!' A beagle dawdled across the road and Mum had to stop.

'A kind of gallery,' I said, looking out my side, and 'there's a shop with a lot of stuff in the window, teddy bears and stuff.'

'There's a Thai restaurant,' Maggie said. 'Hallelujah, Rain — a Thai restaurant!'

'And a pub,' I said. 'And what's that huge place on the corner?'

'A Bed and Breakfast,' Mum said, 'and a bar — well, Clarkson has expanded.'

'It's hardly Chadstone shopping centre,' I said.

'Still, a Thai restaurant. And look, that must be the doctor's place, behind the hedge, and here we are.'

Mum got out of the car and stood with her hands on her hips. 'Needs painting. Definitely needs painting. These cottages scrub up well with a paint job. Look at Granny's roses, Rain — they'll make a beautiful show in summer.'

'Great.'

It was dark inside the house and cold. Both the lounge room and the kitchen were dark and dingy. The bedrooms were better — quite large and with windows that looked out on to the garden.

'Your choice,' Maggie said. 'Which one would you like?'

'This one,' I said, choosing the smallest one, closest to the kitchen, 'I want this one.'

'Are you sure you don't want the bigger one? What about your desk?'

'Can't I have a study in the room next door?' I asked. 'This room?'

'Oh, yes — that's where Granny used to work,' Maggie said. 'It's a lovely warm room, Rain — and look, the plum trees. And spring bulbs coming up, too.'

The house meandered out the back into a large room which had been built on to the original cottage.

'What will we do here?' I asked. 'It's weird, Mum — like a second living room or something.'

'I think it was a family room, originally, ' Mum called out from the kitchen. 'Granny lived down there in winter — don't you remember reading beside her? Oh god, that's what he meant by getting wood in and cooking.'

'What?'

'Mother had a slow combustion stove. I had completely forgotten. I nagged and nagged at her to get a proper stove but she wouldn't. Well, chickadee, it's pizza tonight.'

'What? There isn't a stove?' I was shocked.

'There's a wood stove, a slow combustion stove.' Maggie sounded tired.

'How do you cook on that?'

We looked at it. It was a large stove but it didn't look as though it would ever work.

'I don't know, really,' Maggie said. 'I mean, you put the wood in, obviously, and there are controls to regulate the heat somehow. Mother used to say that nothing cooked bread or soup as well as a slow combustion cooker. I'll have to look it up on the Internet, or ask someone.'

She pulled open the oven door and peered in.

'It doesn't look very clean,' she muttered. 'Oh yuck. I think that's mouse poo.'

'Gross. Forget it, I'm not eating anything cooked in that.'

'Don't be ridiculous.' Mum stood up and glared at me. 'It just needs cleaning.'

'Everything needs cleaning,' I said. 'Everything looks dirty. Even the walls.'

'Shh, isn't that the truck?' Maggie said. 'Go out and have a look, Rain.'

Even our furniture didn't make the house seem brighter.

'Just needs some paint,' Jeff's father said. 'You'll get it right, Mrs Carr. A lick of paint and you won't know the place.'

'There's only a slow combustion cooker,' Mum said.

'With mouse poo in the oven,' I said.

'A good clean out, that's all that needs. There's nothing like these cookers. And this one isn't that old.

I remember the old lady, sorry, I mean your mum, pulling the other one out. This one would be, let's see — she got it a couple of years before she died. They last a lifetime. The old one would have, too. I told her that but she wanted a new one. A fancier one. Look, this one's even got a wok burner. She was proud of that. A great one for cooking, your mum, not like some of these pensioners living on dog food. She'd cook up a nice little meal for herself every night, flowers on the table, the whole bit. People thought she was a bit queer, but I always say live and let live if you're not hurting anyone else.'

'It is a good stove,' Maggie said. 'I remember her getting the brochures.'

'Heats all this part of the house, too,' Jeff's dad said. 'And she could run her hot water from it.'

'So there's no hot water until it's lit?' I couldn't believe what I was hearing.

'Oh there should be. There's gas — if there's any in the bottles.'

'What! Gas in bottles?'

'That's right,' Maggie said, 'you order them from the supermarket. I'd forgotten. They're round the side. There'd be some. You can't move house without needing a bath at the end.'

'There's a bit,' Jeff's dad called through the kitchen window, 'but you'll have to go easy on it. When we've unloaded, Jeff'll go down and order them for you —

they'll deliver 'em Monday — won't do it on the weekend. You'll have to be careful though. I wouldn't run that gas heater if you want a couple of hot baths.'

When they'd emptied the truck, I stood in the gloomy kitchen and looked around. I wanted Maggie to admit that it was all a big mistake, but she didn't. She plugged in the fridge and turned it on. She unpacked a box marked 'Electrical Appliances' and brought out the kettle, the coffee grinder, the blender and the rice cooker. She set these up on the largest bench. She said, 'I'm not going to unpack much, Rain. Not in here. I think we need to do some thinking next week.'

I wondered what she was going to think about — moving back to Brunswick?

'Couldn't we go on renting this house out?' I asked. 'And couldn't we rent a house in the city with the money we got in rent? We wouldn't have to unpack anything then. We'd just ring up Jeff's dad and they could take it all back to the city.'

'Good heavens, darling — the rent we'd get for this wouldn't cover a dog kennel in Melbourne. No, Rain — I meant thinking about what paint colours we want, whether we want to get rid of this lino, what we need to make this house into our special wonderful home.'

'A demolition team,' I said, but very quietly.

The next thing Maggie unpacked was our fridge poetry kit.

'Here we are, Rain — feels like home already! Do you want to put them on?'

Fran had bought the poetry kit on her last overseas trip. It was just a plastic box containing a lot of magnetic words. You stuck these to the fridge and turned them into poetry. It was neat. You don't always have the word you want, though — like our kit has no 'love' in it. And then it's got words that you think you'd never want to use, like 'kill'.

Mum and I wrote poems to each other. Not soppy poems. We wrote about stuff that maybe we don't want to actually talk about. I like poetry. I was named after a poem, after all. Everyone thinks I'm called Rain because I have dippy hippy parents, but that is actually not the case at all. Before Mum became Maggie she was an education administrator who wore high-heeled shoes and had her hair done every six weeks by Jodie at The Do to Die For. And Dad's a systems network architect, which is to do with computers, not buildings, and he wears a suit to work every day.

I was named after a line from a poem. It was by e e cummings, who wasn't into capital letters. I had just been born, Mum said, and she knocked the basinette I was sleeping in and I startled. Which is what they call it when babies open their hands up wide, like little stars. Mum knew then I would be Rain — 'nobody, not even the rain, has such small hands'.

Rain was a good name for Brunswick, Melbourne, where everyone is dippy hippy, post-punk or wired techno, but I wasn't sure it was going to be such a great name in Clarkson, Central Victoria, where Jeff's dad said 'wok' as though it was a word he hadn't heard much before.

It was depressing to even think of, so I checked out the garden. Maggie was right — it was a great garden. I remembered more and more about it as I explored. It's funny about memories, how they suddenly plonk into your mind, and it is as though once they start you can't stop them. First I remembered gathering damson plums with Granny. She would pull down the branches and I'd pluck the plums off for her, into a big bucket. Then I remembered eating bread warm from the oven spread with plum jam. Then I remembered her scrubbing my face until it shone like an apple and felt warm from my forehead to my chin. I was muddy — I'd been playing in the new vegetable garden bed. The bed was still there, although it was totally overgrown with weeds.

Right along the fence were apple trees, their branches stretched out so they were almost horizontal to the fence, like prisoners being tortured. I wandered over to look at the hard, new little apples and remembered Granny walking along the fence and naming each tree for me. 'Gravenstein, you don't get your Gravenstein apple in a supermarket. The best crisp apple in the world.' Then I remembered eating the apples she baked in a buttery, golden sauce.

I was getting hungry, when I got that 'someone's watching you' feeling and looked around.

'Up here,' a weedy voice said, and I looked up and straight into a boy's face. He was in a tree-house next door, a tree-house which looked right over Granny's — I mean our — backyard.

'You've just moved,' he said.

'Brilliant,' I said. 'As if you have to be Einstein to work that one out.'

'How old are you?'

'Nearly thirteen,' I said, crossing my fingers behind my back. I was actually just twelve years and one month old. 'How old are you?' He looked younger than me. His hair was all thick and sticking up and his face was a pale triangle against the dark wood. He was thin, too.

'I'm just about eleven and a half,' he said, 'but I'm phenomenally bright. What's your name?'

'Rain May Carr-Davies,' I said.

'Rain?' he said. 'Like that girl in *Future's End, Star Trek, Voyager* series?'

I didn't know what he was talking about. 'After an e e cummings poem, actually,' I said.

'Oh.' He sounded a little disappointed. 'That's a

shame. She's quite a good minor character even if she does go all soppy over Lieutenant Tom Parish in the end. I'm named after a biblical figure. I'm Daniel. Daniel Stephen Gill.'

'Right,' I said. 'So is your dad or your mum the doctor?'

'My father is,' Daniel said. 'Counsellor Diana helps out in reception sometimes, but mostly she worries.'

'She's a counsellor?'

'No, I just call her that. She's empathetic, like Counsellor Troy from *Star Trek*.'

'What is all this *Star Trek* stuff? What are you talking about?'

'Television show,' he said patiently. 'Mr Spock. Movies, too. Haven't you ever heard of it?'

'No.'

'Pity. So what do you do?'

'What do you mean?'

'I mean, do you play chess, collect stamps, go bushwalking, play basketball, or do you just muck around?'

Daniel's question made me feel as though I should do something wonderfully original to impress him, although I wasn't sure why.

'I write fridge poetry,' I said, suddenly inspired, 'and I should really be unpacking.'

'Fridge poetry?'

'You know, it's what everyone's doing in America these days.'

It was Daniel's turn to sound unsure.

'Do you just write it on the fridge?' he said. 'You mean with textas?'

'No, stupid, you get a kit of magnetic words.'

'So you stick the words up on the fridge and they make poems?'

'Yeah.'

'Can I come over and have a go?'

'Well, maybe later, maybe when we're unpacked. Probably tomorrow?'

'Hey, that'd be neat. Thanks.'

'I'd better go now,' I said. 'We have loads and loads of stuff to unpack.'

'Yeah. Counsellor Diana said that moving was really tough. She was going to bring your mum over some soup because she said you'd never get that big old slow combustion stove working and what if you didn't have a microwave, but Dad said city people might think that a little strange. What will you have for dinner, though, that's what I want to know.'

'Pizza, Mum said.'

'From where?'

'We'll get it delivered,' I said. 'That's what we did at home if Maggie worked late.'

'You can't get it delivered here,' Daniel said. 'Where would it come from?'

'Well the pizza place, stupid, I mean where else?'

'There isn't a pizza place in town,' Daniel said, 'so stupid yourself.'

'No pizza place?'

'Nup. Closed down. They went to Queensland.'

'You're joking?' I said. 'That is so horrible. No pizza place. I knew we shouldn't have moved. I just knew it. I'd better tell Mum.'

'See you tomorrow,' Daniel called out as I trudged up to the house, but I was too discouraged to do more than just give him a tiny wave without even turning around.

'There's no pizza place,' I said to Mum. 'Maggie, we're going to starve.'

'We don't eat that much pizza, Rain.'

'Tonight, though, we'll have absolutely nothing to eat. The woman next door, the doctor's wife? She was going to bring over soup but Daniel's father said we'd think that was strange so we haven't even got that.'

'Who is Daniel?'

'Their son. He's eleven and a half and phenomenally bright.'

'*Phenomenally* bright?'

'That's what he said. Mum, what are we going to do about dinner?'

'We'll go down to the supermarket and get some-thing — baked beans. I don't know, Rain. How's your room? Can we concentrate on what needs to be done, please?'

In the end we didn't even make it to the supermarket. It closed at 5.00 pm on weekends. We nearly didn't make it to the fish and chip shop. It closed at 7.30 pm and we got there a minute before. The chips were soggy.

'Disgusting,' I said, 'absolutely inedible.' But I ate them anyway, because there wasn't anything else.

'Who would have thought the supermarket would close so early?' Maggie said. 'Not that I expect to shop here — the prices were always horrendous. I think I might drive to Bendigo once a week. Well, I'm done in. I'm going to run a bath — you can hop in after me, Rain — that way we won't waste any hot water.'

'You mean in the same water?'

'Yes, of course.'

'But Mum, all your skin will be in the bath. There'll be a sludge of dead skin cells floating on the water.'

'I don't think you need to worry about dead skin cells tonight. Just for one night.'

She was right. There were worse things ahead. The house made so many unfamiliar noises that I couldn't get to sleep for the longest time. And when I did finally drift off, someone thumping around on the roof woke me up and I screamed out wildly.

'It's a possum,' Mum called, 'that's all. Possums in

the roof. We'll have to get them out somehow. They can damage the wiring and wee up there.'

I looked up at my ceiling. In one corner, right above my bed, was a round stain I hadn't noticed before. 'It's done it,' I shouted. 'It's peed above my bed.'

'Rain!'

'Mum, it has. It'll probably leak down during the night. I'll get possum pee in my eyes and up my nose. Please, please can I come in with you?'

Mum appeared at my door. She was wearing her saggy, sleepy face. She peered up where I pointed.

'I don't think that's possum pee,' she said. 'I think that might be a rain leak, or something. Anyway, it's not fresh. I wouldn't worry.'

'Please Mum,' I said, 'I don't like the night here. It's too noisy. My heart is still thumping all over the place.'

'Noisy?' she said. 'After the traffic on Sydney Road? Oh come on, then. Just keep your dead skin on your side, all right?'

Mum's room already smelled like home because she'd burnt some incense in her little brass burner. She had unpacked some books, too, and they lay on her bedside table as though she had been reading them all week. The room looked friendly. It had been waiting for her, I decided sleepily. Maybe the whole house had been waiting for us. Maybe it could be the best Maggie-and-Rain house just like Mum promised.

I nearly got out of bed and changed my moving-day

fridge poem, which was only small but packed in a lot of bitterness and had been inspired by the lack of pizza. I didn't though. It was too cold out there in the middle of the night. I thought I'd get up early in the morning and change it before Maggie even noticed.

I thought that maybe when Dad got sick of Julia and executive stress he'd come up and like the house so much he'd move back in. He and Maggie would fall in love again and watch television at night holding hands and kiss in the commercial breaks like teenagers and that would be really sick. Maybe Daniel has an older, gorgeous brother who would fall in love with me when I turn fourteen and we'd get married and open a groovy Brunswick kind of pizza place in Clarkson and everyone would say it was a great day for Clarkson when Rain May Carr-Davies-Gill moved in to town.

Moving Day Fridge Poem

me
cleaned out
homeless
girl
everything about me
decay
I am haunted
and asking
why

Maggie's Reply

celebrate grass
       tree
        cloud
no concrete
every day
can laugh
and will heal
we are secretly feline
our slow rhythms
flower brilliantly

o crap
have a bath

The Captain's Log, Stardate 130901 —
Winter's End, Alpha Quadrant

Counsellor Diana just informed Dr McGarvis to expect alien activity on Planet 7 tomorrow. New settlers are arriving. This is bad news as it means the back territory will be out of bounds again but good news as all change brings with it new potentials.

The people moving in actually own the place — the old woman's daughter, she said — rather than more tenants. The Ferengi at the supermarket told her. They know everything. I suspect young Mr Stewart has a link to the police computer equipment. He probably has his mobile phone tuned to their frequency. Not that I think the alien activity will be closely observed by our security officers.

I can't actually remember the old woman dying — well, that's not so surprising, is it? She died there — let me just check with Mum — yep, about four years ago. Planet 7 wasn't under surveillance by the USS *Endeavour* then. In fact, that was the year I collected stamps. Or was it the year I panned for gold? Anyway, sometime later the first aliens arrived. They didn't stay long. Too cold, they said, atmosphere hostile, nutrients expensive, company dismal, and they moved up the highway. Pity, they had a son who played chess, like me, and, like me, hated sport.

The next colonisers were a dead loss, too. A couple

of girls, practically teenagers. All they did was sit out in the sun all day and paint their toenails and dry their hair. They were living away from the mother ship for the first time. Males of their species kept arriving in hotted-up starships and driving recklessly away long after my bedtime.

Then there was the strange alien, the one we simply had to place under surveillance because he was so unreadable. That's when Planet 7 got its name and that's when I started this Log. Despite all my efforts, I could find no reason why he shouldn't stay on Planet 7 and do his work. It turned out, after months of close watching, that he was an artist, that was all. Of course this rather shocked the larger population of Cosmos, but I'm afraid that's what Cosmos is like — a system occupied by the mediocre, the plain stupid, the incurious and the aged. Present company excepted, of course.

The Captain's Log, Stardate 140901

The aliens arrived. Both females. One is Counsellor Diana's age, the other is more my age. I climbed the observation tower knowing that the smaller female would eventually check out the back territory. I was not disappointed. First contact was friendly.

Her name's Rain, not after the astronomer in *Future's End*, *Star Trek*, *Voyager*, Season 3, but after a poem. She's heavily into poetry. She writes fridge poetry. I don't know anyone who writes poetry. They tried to make us do it at school but the Klingons wrote obscene limericks instead.

Counsellor Diana thought about taking them soup. The Doctor said they might think that strange, though. She should have gone ahead — Rain thought they could get home-delivered pizza! Boy, she will take some acclimatising to Cosmos.

I wonder if she plays chess? I wonder if she'll want to be friends, even though I'm a boy and younger?

Counsellor Diana said not to expect too much from the aliens. She said their ways may be different. She said they may not even stay. People do rather tend to leave Cosmos. I have noticed this. It could be the hostile environment, the lack of sufficient entertainment pods and employment for young colonisers.

I hope they do stay. I'd be friends with any kid next door within a reasonable age range. Their gender wouldn't worry me. Anyway, if she's as old as she said, why isn't she taller? And why hasn't she got female signs developing? She looked just like a boy. And she's not much taller than I am.

I think the alien lied about her age.

I hope the alien lied about her age. I hope she's not a snobby city girly girl. There are lots of things I could show her that might interest her — the platypus in the river, the best yabbying place, the McMaster alpacas and where Dad and I saw the echidna last month.

Two minutes until lights extinguished and sleep pod activated. Lights still burning on Ship 7. I wonder if she's up writing on the fridge? Poets work at night, I believe. One minute and Counsellor Diana is counting down. Yes, yes — good night, Mum. Good night, galaxy. Lights off.

The Captain's Log. Stardate 150901

Fridge poetry was frustrating. The words you want are not there. Maggie, that's Rain's commander-in-chief, said it didn't have to rhyme, but it sounds better when it does, I reckon. Anyway, what I think is that they've evolved it into a highly selective language of their own. There are hidden messages. A useful communication device that at first glance appears lame.

Commander-in-chief Maggie talks to you as though you're nearly at her rank. That could be a sophisticated alien ploy — assimilate or die. It sounds like they are staying, though — she was pretty keen on getting the place painted and she wanted to know all about the Training Barracks. I didn't tell them it was like Hades, only noisier. What was the point. She'll find out soon enough.

Observations of Artefacts on Ship 7

1. *Small* visual entertainment unit — indicating a wider acceptance of printed material than generally regarded as normal on Cosmos.
2. *No* computer!
3. Many of the small female alien's printed visual stimuli match my own. And she's in the same year as me, so she did lie about her age.
4. Little or no evidence of girl artefacts such as nail polish, glitter gel etcetera.
5. CHESS SET! But pieces in an old jar and no board visible.

They didn't seem to mind me hanging round, observing. They didn't shoo me away or ask me whether I hadn't anything better to do. If they had, the answer would have been 'no'. The Doctor is on hospital duty and Counsellor Diana is out doing good. It's her old-people day. She'll come home with a knitted vest for me from Mrs Gregor — some strange colour mix. Her eyesight's worse, the Doctor says. I'll have to wear it. What I want is one of those vests that are waterproof with lots of different pockets. That would be useful.

And she'll have a couple of jars of jam or pickles from Mrs Doherty — they'll be yummy and she dates all hers so you know if it's really too old to eat, not like Mr Wills'. He doesn't bother and he can never remember which year he made them. The last lot I reckon might have been made when his wife was still alive — and she's been dead three years. I told Mum not to bother — just throw them straight in the bin — but she will open them and there was mould, right over the whole top. Disgusting.

She'll be exhausted, too, and headachey. The Doctor will pour her a glass of wine. I saw him put a bottle in the fridge before he left this morning. He'll tell her she shouldn't visit them, it's not her responsibility. And they'll talk about the old days, when there was a proper community. Then she'll watch television and the Doctor and I will play chess.

There's the landing vehicle.

Later: 2000 hours

The Doctor narrowly checkmated me. I do not play a good defence game. It's a weakness. Also my openings are stale. I wish there was a chess club here so I could really practise. Can't wait until high school. They have a club there and play chess in the lunch hours when it's rainy. That could be a lot of chess in winter and spring. Age and strength don't matter with chess. Your mind is all. I do have a good mind. Otherwise the Upper Training Barracks would not have approved my early promotion. Depending on health evaluation, as the Counsellor and the Doctor remind me.

Sleep pod in ten minutes. Captain Daniel is retiring to revise chess strategies. Next week the championship returns to me!

The Dream House Countdown

Making Granny's old place into the dream house wasn't easy. For a start we had to drive practically all the way back home to get the kind of paint we wanted. That took one whole day because Maggie insisted on doing a big grocery shop as well, then we had to check out the op shops, then she had to have a cup of coffee. It was all right for Maggie, but I was on a tight schedule. I wanted our house fixed up quickly, like they do on those television shows. The owners go away for the weekend and hey presto! your dumpy old backyard is now an outdoor Balinese temple.

The way I saw it was we'd blitz the house and when Dad came to pick me up on Friday for the weekend he'd stand there gaping at the work we'd done and remember all the reasons he shouldn't have left Mum. It's not that I don't like Julia, mind you, it's just that she really had no right to walk off with Dad. Of course,

I couldn't tell Mum my plan, because she'd go off on one of her 'embrace change' rants and stroke my hair in that way she does when she's telling me I'm a goose. So Mum was in no hurry at all.

She spent most of the second day reading a book on painted effects and asking me dumb questions like whether I thought the Tuscan look would enhance the kitchen or whether it would just look badly painted. I made her start on my room after lunch by threatening to paint it myself if she read for much longer.

I thought I'd like painting. I thought it would be a matter of whacking the paint on over the revolting dirty cream and, whammo, there would be my new purple bedroom looking gorgeous. No such luck. First of all we had to wash down the walls. Then we had to sand them back. Then Mum fussed around putting sheets over everything, as if we were going to really slop the paint around. Then we had to stir the paint one hundred and one times to make sure it was all mixed in. Only then did Mum fill the roller tray and let us start.

Once we started though, the room was done pretty quickly. The paint was Dream Rhapsody, a kind of purpley violet colour. I had wanted Violet Moon, but Mum said that was too dark and I'd feel as though I was living in a gothic cave. That sounded cool to me, but Mum said the one thing that would get you down in winter was living in a gloomy purple cave and that it would be simply impossible to paint over so I would be stuck with it forever and ever.

Dream Rhapsody was pretty good, though, and she was right, the room looked like the inside of a shell when we'd finished.

'We'll have to do another coat tomorrow,' Maggie said, standing back to look at it, hands on her hips, 'and then we'll do all the skirting boards and the picture rails that darker purple. It'll be great, Rain.'

Inspired by our success we checked out the grim front room with its dreadful carpet.

'I think we should just pull the carpet up,' Maggie said. 'I'll bet there are good floor boards underneath this. Can you find me a hammer?'

The carpet was so old it practically disintegrated as Maggie pulled up the strips of wood that held it in place along one wall. Underneath it was a pile of dirt and sand.

'That's disgusting,' I said.

'That's why people say that carpets give you asthma,' Maggie said. 'Come on, you tug this bit out and then bring me a knife, a big one, and we'll see if we can't cut up some of the underlay.'

By the end of Day Two of the renovations, we had the first coat of my room done and the lounge-room carpet ripped up. We'd emptied the vacuum cleaner five times, and whenever I blew my nose, my snot came out black. Fortunately our gas bottles had been delivered so we could both have a hot bath. I didn't see Maggie's bath water, but mine was murky brown by the time I got out.

I was so exhausted that I didn't even hear the possum that night. When Maggie came out the next morning, though, practically the first thing she did was ring National Parks and Wildlife.

'With the racket that thing is making,' she said, 'it sounds as though it's having wild parties up there with all its possum friends.'

So the next day was spent discovering how to de-possum the roof. And it wasn't easy. You could get a cage, but relocation was tricky. You couldn't just take it out to the forest and hope it would survive. Other possums could attack it.

'So what do we do?' Maggie said. 'I mean, I'm practically a vegetarian. I wouldn't want to hurt anything, really, but I can't endure another night of the jackbooted little monsters.'

Apparently there was nothing for it except to trap the possum to get it out of the roof, block the holes where it was getting in, and purchase a possum house to put in a tree in the garden which might, with some fruity inducements, provide an alternative shelter. That way the possum remained in its own territory and, providing your roof was properly fixed, wouldn't damage the wiring or keep you awake at night. We drove off to rent a possum trap and buy a possum house.

The trap was a large wire cage with a tricky door arrangement at one end. You stuck an apple on this bit and when the possum tugged at the apple the door shut behind it, neatly trapping it in the cage.

'Or that's the theory,' Maggie said, looking at it with suspicion. 'And that's if we can get the darn thing up in the roof.'

The possum houses were made by a skinny man with a pigtail and an earring in one ear.

'So you've moved into your mum's house,' he said, coming out to greet us in the driveway. 'Good solid little house that. My dad built the family room at the back.'

'We want a possum house,' Maggie said.

'Yeah, in the roof, are they? Once they're there it's a devil's job to get them out. But it's our fault, you know, felling trees in the Wombat State Forest, keeping these greedy wood-gulping slow combustion heaters going. People going out and picking up all the dead wood to save money — think they're doing the environment a good turn, too, but little creatures depend on that dead wood. Hollow logs, you see — all sorts of creatures live in them. Still, we do the best we can.'

'Yes,' Maggie said, 'yes we do. How much are they, please?'

The possum house looked like a tiny little house,

complete with roof. The 'doorway' though, was round, to imitate the hollow logs, I suppose.

'Got a ladder?' Pete asked, leaning against the side of Maggie's car, as though the effort involved in selling us a possum house had exhausted him.

'Yes,' Maggie said. She was not in a chatty mood.

Securing the possum house in the Japanese maple tree was impossible. First of all we tried to just wedge it between two branches, but that simply didn't work.

'Well, I don't know,' Maggie said, looking at the beautiful little house on the ground at our feet. 'I just can't work it out. The darn thing will have to learn to live on the ground, that's all.'

'Excuse me, excuse me,' a voice from Daniel's side of the fence called out, and Mum and I turned to see Daniel's mum looking at us.

'Hi,' she said, 'I'm sorry to intrude, although I believe Daniel already has. I do hope he wasn't a nuisance.'

'Not at all.' Maggie smiled her meeting-other-mothers smile. 'A delightful boy.'

'Thank you. Look, about the possum house, I think I can help. You see, you build a platform first. I can see just the spot from here. If you wouldn't mind me coming over, I have tools.'

'Mind?' Maggie said. 'Oh, if only you would. I tell you, I'd buy this possum a unit on the Gold Coast if I thought I could get it to move out of my roof.'

'Have you rung Bob about the roof?'

'Bob?'

'Your mother always used Bob, he's a very good handyman. Quite reasonable too. I'll get his number. Do you mind if Daniel comes over too? School holidays — well, of course, you know.'

'No, of course not, please bring him.'

Within about five minutes Daniel and his mother were standing in our yard with planks of wood, a jar of nails and a small saw. Our mothers murmured names to each other and then shook hands. Over her slim jeans and blouse, Daniel's mother wore a professional carpenter's apron.

'Mum built the tree-house,' Daniel said.

'Gosh Diana, did you really. That's fantastic.'

Diana seemed to go a little pinker in her cheeks. When she smiled, her face changed completely. It was as though the smile chased away all the little worry lines from around her eyes and mouth.

'I love mucking around with wood and nails,' she said. 'Very unladylike. I built all our kitchen cupboards. They thought I was mad, but honestly, Maggie, those cupboards sing to me every day. The drawers slide in and out, there's no room behind anything for mice to nest, and the bench height is right where I need it.'

'I know this is forward of me,' Maggie said, 'but do you reckon we could have a look? We're renovating my mother's old house, Rain and I. Just checking out other people's places can be so helpful.'

'Of course, of course, you must come in. Let's just get this dear little house up in the tree. You give Bob a ring and tell him Diana said he has to come today. He's not that busy in winter, anyway.'

Mum went off to see if she could locate Bob.

'How's the poetry?' Daniel asked me.

'The poetry?'

'Yeah, your fridge poetry?'

'Oh, good. I haven't done much lately. We've been painting and ripping up old carpet.'

'Yes, I saw that. Counsellor Diana said they should be great floor boards under that old stuff. She wondered if you had an orbital sander or if you were getting someone in to do it?'

'I don't think we've got a sander,' I said. 'I don't know what Mum's going to do. We only ripped it up yesterday. We're trying to get as much as possible done to show Dad on the weekend.'

'Oh, does he come up on the weekend?'

'No. I go to his place. He and Mum don't live together at the moment.'

'Oh. Do you miss him?'

'Sort of.'

'Pass me some nails, love,' Daniel's mum said. She had measured some wood up, cut it, and was now nailing a bottom slat on to keep the paling platform together. It was amazing how alike they were, Daniel and his mum. They both had gingery wavy hair, pale faces and freckles. Like Daniel, his mother was short and slight, her wrists so small they made the hammer look larger than it was.

By the time Maggie came back out, the possum house was up snugly on its little platform looking like a smaller version of Daniel's tree-house. I knew what Mum had been busy doing — washing up the breakfast dishes and generally tidying up. Sure enough, when we all trooped into the kitchen it was sparkly, as far as it could be with boxes of our stuff shoved up against one wall.

'Oh, isn't it warm in here.' Diana immediately drew her chair up closer to the stove. 'So how is the move going, Maggie?'

'Slowly,' Maggie said. 'So far we've painted Rain's room and ripped up the carpet. What I'd like to do is get rid of all the carpet while we're at it, before we settle in too much. Once you've got everything down, that's the end. You never get round to it.'

'It must be hard doing it by yourself, too.' Diana looked around the kitchen.

Maggie frowned. 'It is in some ways,' she said, 'but I don't have to please anyone other than myself. And Rain, of course, but she's not that interested in kitchens.'

'If there's anything I can do,' Diana said. 'Really, I love this kind of thing and I'm home mostly.'

'Mum likes projects,' Daniel said. 'Can Rain come to our house? Mum's made chocolate cake.'

'Daniel!'

'Would you like a cup of tea?' Maggie said. 'Or coffee?'

'I'd love tea, if you've time, but otherwise, it's fine. Daniel, sweetie, why don't you take Rain to our place and have a piece of cake each. That way Rain's mother and I can get acquainted.'

Diana's chocolate cake was heaven in a slice. It was rich and crumbly and she'd iced it.

'It's a wonder you're not fat,' I said to Daniel, my mouth wickedly full.

'She doesn't cook like this all the time,' Daniel said. 'You've got to make the most of it. Another slice?'

You could only eat two slices of Diana's chocolate cake. We tried to get up to three, but we could only manage a mouse bite of the third slices.

'We'll just cut the corners off,' Daniel said, 'and it'll look as though we had trouble cutting it.'

'Which is your room?' I asked.

'Come and I'll show you around.'

Daniel's house was huge, far bigger than ours. There was even an office at the front, with its own fireplace.

'Dad works here,' Daniel whispered, pulling the door shut quickly, 'and this is their bedroom.'

I had an impression of pale colours and extreme tidiness before that door, too, was closed.

'And this is my room.' Daniel threw himself on the bed. I had to practically duck — every inch of ceiling space was taken up with hanging aeroplane models. 'That's a Cessna,' he said, as one of them swung a little wildly and hit me in the head. 'Watch out, they aren't that strong.'

'They're great,' I said. 'Do you make them?'

'Counsellor Diana and I do. We're building up to a model of the *Enterprise*. I think we'll have to order one from the States though.'

'Is that another *Star Trek* thing?'

'That's their craft, stupid.'

'Why doesn't your father make them with you?'

Daniel shrugged. 'He doesn't do this kind of stuff. He doesn't have time. He's practically always on call and always rushing out in the night.'

'My dad's pretty busy, too,' I said.

'But he doesn't even live with you.'

'No, but he was busy when he did. He'll probably move back, when he sees what we've done to the house.'

'So what, he moved out so you could fix the house?'

'Sort of,' I said.

'So is he living in your old place?'

'No. At a friend's.'

'Right. What do you want to play?'

'I don't know.'

'Do you play chess?'

'Yes, sort of. I'm not very good, though.'

'I'm very good,' Daniel said. 'Dad and I play some-times. We keep a game going in his surgery. They can take weeks to finish.'

Three games of chess later, I heard Mum's voice in the kitchen, admiring Diana's cupboards, drawers and her chocolate cake.

'You'll have to improve,' Daniel said, setting up another game, 'then we can play properly. And you will, Rain, you'll get better. I was nearly as bad as you, but I just kept playing and thinking about my game and reading books.'

I wasn't sure that I wanted to read books on chess but I was darn sure I wanted to beat Daniel one day. It was bad enough losing to a boy, but losing to a boy who was younger than me and so horribly confident really riled me. The thing about Daniel, I was learning, was that he was utterly matter-of-fact about his abilities. He didn't actually boast, even though it may have sounded like that. He just told the truth. He told the truth about his weaknesses, too.

I lost another game of chess and then Maggie came and we walked home together.

'Well, that's a plus,' Mum said. 'What a lovely woman. Stressed to the max, obviously. Did you see the house, Rain, not a thing out of place. You know, that kind of obsessive housekeeping can be more stressful than anything else. It's so meaningless. And when you think she made all those cupboards herself. She could be a carpenter. She could be out there renovating houses — she's coming in tomorrow and we're going to do the kitchen with that Tuscan look I showed you. She thinks it will look beautiful. Then we might drive to Bendigo. She thinks we could redo all the bench tops with jarrah floor boards.'

Maggie and I loaded the possum trap that night with an apple smeared with honey. That was the easy part. Getting it up in the roof was more difficult. I had to wait until Maggie squeezed through the little access hole and then, standing on the ladder, I lifted the cage up to her. It was heavy and my arms ached. When Maggie finally came down, covered in cobwebs, she was grinning triumphantly.

'We did it, Rain, all by ourselves. Don't you feel proud?'

We had a cup of hot chocolate to celebrate and went to bed. I lay awake for ages listening, but I didn't hear as much as a possum sneeze.

Maggie woke me when I'd just got to sleep, or that's what it felt like. It was still dark and I didn't know what she was doing pulling my shoulder like that when it wasn't even a school day. I'd been dreaming about my old school and hanging out with Emma and

Lisa and I'd forgotten that Emma had gone to Sydney and that we'd moved, too.

'Wake up,' Maggie said urgently. 'Rain, you have to wake up.'

'All right,' I said, trying to open my eyes, which felt heavy as rocks, 'what's the time?'

'Four in the morning, but listen, Rain, listen — we got the possum!'

I shut my eyes again and listened. There was a thumping and banging high above me somewhere.

'Good,' I said, 'that's great. Night night.'

'No, Rain, come on — you have to help me. We have to get it down now.'

'No.'

'Yes, come on, darling, wake up.' And she pulled the blankets off me, letting in a rush of icy air.

'Mum!'

'I think,' Maggie said, standing at the bottom of the ladder, 'that you're going to have to get up in the roof, kind of nudge the cage along to the hole and then I'm going to have to get it from here. A full-grown possum in that cage will be too heavy for you. Here's the torch.'

I was scared of spiders and not too keen on going up in the roof, but I was desperate to see the possum.

'Okay, you hold the ladder.'

'Got it.'

Inside the roof was pitch black and then shadowy when I shone the torch around.

'Don't shine the torch in its eyes,' Mum said anxiously from her post on the ladder. 'It'll scare it.'

Once you got used to the dark, it wasn't quite as bad. I covered the torch with my hand and in the faintest light that escaped I could see the possum cowering at the furtherest end of the cage.

'It's okay,' I said quietly, 'you're just moving, like we had to. That's all.'

It was hard moving the cage gently but finally I got it to the edge of the hole. Mum threw up a couple of towels and told me to cover the cage so we didn't blind the possum, as we moved it into the sudden light of the lounge room. While I did this there was a soft scuffle alongside the cage and without thinking I reached down.

The claws were frantic and very sharp.

'Ouch,' I cried and nearly dropped the cage.

'What is it?' Maggie said. 'Not a spider, Rain?'

'No, it's — good heavens, Mum, it's another possum. A baby.'

'Careful darling, they'll fight like crazy, you know. They can kill cats.'

'Not a baby, Mum.'

'Put it in the towel, if you can. Hold on, I'll grab a pillow case.'

I wrapped the terrified baby possum in the towel, all the time talking in a low soothing voice.

Mum's head appeared through the hole.

'Here,' she said, 'I'll hold it open, you put her in.'

Uncermoniously we dumped baby in the pillow case and Mum disappeared, clutching the top of the pillow case tightly. In the cage, the mother possum made a growling sound that rumbled from deep inside her chest. I rubbed at my scratches. It had been worth it, I thought, remembering how soft the baby's fur was.

'Now what?' I asked, clambering down the ladder. 'Where will we put her?'

'I don't know?' Maggie held the pillow case at arm's length, even though the little bundle had stopped thrashing around. 'I just don't think I can get her safely in the cage with her mum. And we can't let either of them out until Bob finishes the roof.'

'A box?' I said. We had a lot of boxes left over from the move. They were stacked everywhere.

'A box? I don't know. I suppose that would be okay as an interim measure. I'm worried that when she calms down she'll try to scratch her way out and the last thing we want is an escaped baby possum. I'm sure there's an old cat cage in the shed. Unless it got turfed. Do you remember Grumpy?'

'No.'

'Mum's old Persian. Ugh, it was the ugliest cat.'

'I can't remember anything,' I said. 'It isn't fair. Can we get a cat?'

'No,' Maggie said firmly, 'I'm having enough problems with wildlife as it is. A cat is not on the agenda.

Let's get a box and then I'll look for something more suitable in the shed.'

We found a sturdy box and Mum dumped the whole pillowcase in it, loosening the top first, of course. We then wrapped masking tape round and round the box, but making sure there were enough air holes for the possum. There was a faint scrabbling sound from within the box and then silence.

'I think they'd be better off in a dark room,' Maggie said. 'Let's put them in your bedroom for the time being, and then you can come in with me for what's left of the night.'

'You think they're okay?' I said. 'You don't think we should give the little one some food or water?'

'No,' Maggie said. 'No, I don't think so. It's only going to be a couple of hours. They'll be fine. Then we'll look for the cage. Bob'll come and finish the roof and we'll let them out at the bottom of the tree with their new ritzy house in it.'

I looked up at Mum. She had dark baggy circles under her eyes, her mouth was pale and her hair looked limp. Even the curly bits at the ends looked as though they were making an effort to stay jaunty. When she bent over and grasped the big possum cage, I could see where her grey hairs were growing out of the dark burgundy dye she used. She was wearing an old t-shirt and her arms were all goosepimpled from the cold.

'I'll take the box,' I offered. 'And I could make you cup of tea?'

'Thanks, but let's just get back to bed, eh?'

It was still totally dark. I pulled aside a little of the curtain in Maggie's room and looked out into the night.

'There's a mist,' I said. 'It looks really pretty.'

Maggie came and stood beside me. 'It's beautiful,' she said softly. 'You know, Granny really liked living here. I remember when she first moved and how I'd bring you up as a little baby. They were such peaceful times, Rain. She loved you so much. Watching her with you made me realise how much she loved me.'

The dark made it easier to talk, somehow, and back in the warm snug of Maggie's bed I felt able to ask, casually, as though it had just occurred to me, when Dad was picking me up on Friday.

'He won't come all the way here,' Maggie said, sounding surprised. 'I'll take you down to Sunbury, that's roughly halfway. He'll pick you up there.'

'So he's not coming up here at all?'

'Not at this stage, no. There's no need. Anyway, there's a few things I can get at Sunbury.'

'I thought he'd want to see the house, what we've done.' I couldn't help saying that, even though I knew it was the wrong thing to say.

There was a long silence and then Maggie said, slowly, 'Rain, this house has nothing to do with Dad.

My life, now, except for where you are concerned, has nothing to do with Dad.'

'I just thought he'd like to see what we've done,' I said, even though I knew I shouldn't.

'I don't particularly want him to see what we've done,' Maggie said. 'I want a clear space where he hasn't been. You can take photos of your room, if you like, but this house is mine.'

'I thought — it doesn't matter.'

'Rain, do you remember the fights? Do you remember your dad driving off in the night? Do you remember us forever yelling at each other? The crying, the endless, endless shouting and griping and accusations?'

'It wasn't always like that,' I said. 'Remember going to St Kilda, eating fish and chips on the beach? Dad teaching me to roller blade?'

'I remember going to St Kilda and you and I sitting on the beach waiting for him to come back from Julia's place. I remember him deciding to take up roller blading because he wanted to lose some weight because Julia said he was developing a paunch. I remember …'

'I don't want to hear anymore,' I said. 'I don't want to hear anymore.'

'I'm sorry, Rain, I'm really sorry.' Maggie found my hand in the dark and held it. 'It's not that he's a bad man, sweetheart, it's just that this kind of stuff happens. And of course, you are absolutely right, there are lots of good things to remember. And you still have him, he's still your dad. He'll never not be that, Rain. He loves you enormously and you're never to forget that. It's just that he's your dad-with-Julia now and I'm Maggie, your mother, living in the country. You'll get the best of both, chickadee — the Melbourne latte society promenading where it's good to be seen on a Sunday morning and then possum-catching and walking in the Wombat State Forest quietly so as not to disturb the blue tongue lizards or the roos.'

'I know, Mum, I'm sorry.' I didn't know what I was really saying sorry for, whether for raising the whole subject or not being totally happy with the idea of living in two different places with parents who didn't live together the way I knew they should, the way they'd promised to in the photos Maggie had put away.

'Go back to sleep now,' Maggie whispered and she stroked my hair back from my forehead, the way she did when I had flu. 'Sleepy Rain, sleepy possums, sleepy stars, back to sleep before the sun wakes up.'

It wasn't that I didn't care about the house now I knew that Dad wouldn't be seeing it, it was just that I was tired and there was nothing I could really do. Mum was busy banging down nail heads in the floor in the lounge room, Bob was hammering away outside the roof, and I was forbidden to go next door to even ask

Daniel over to look at the possums until there was visible stirring.

At ten o'clock, Daniel's mum went outside with a load of washing and hung it on the line and I scooted over to the fence.

'We caught the possums,' I told her. 'A mother and a baby. We put the baby in a box but then Mum found the old cat cage in the shed and we transferred it to that. It nearly got out but we were quicker and Mum grabbed it. The mother possum has already eaten some apple. Mum reckons we could probably feed them a little fruit, just at first, while they settle in to their new home. Can Daniel come and see them, please?'

'Of course, darling, he'll love that. And tell your mum I'll be over in a tick, when I've done the vacuuming.'

'Does your mother vacuum every day,' I asked Daniel after we'd quietly been in to see the possums and put more apple in their cages.

'I don't know,' he said. 'I suppose so. There are things called dust mites, you know. They live on your skin. We shed skin all the time and they eat it. And there can be lead in carpets, too. And pesticides. Counsellor Diana read an article on it in the *New Scientist*. So, yeah, I reckon she probably vacuums to get rid of it all. She wanted to rip up the carpets like your mum's doing but the Doctor said it was too much work for her and he hasn't got round to it yet. Do you want to go down to the river?'

'Are you allowed?'

'Strictly speaking?' Daniel asked quietly. 'Well, only to certain bits, the more boring bits, if you ask me. The bits where the platypuses are Diana says are too deep and anything can happen if you're there by yourself. But you see, I wouldn't be by myself, would I? You'd be there. So logically, we'd be able to go there because we'd be with each other. Anyway, I can swim. Can you?'

'Of course.'

'Well, you tell your mum,' Daniel said. 'I think she's less nervous than the Counsellor. You tell her we're going exploring and we'll be back for lunch. They like it when you tell them when you'll be back.'

'Have you got a watch?'

'Yep.' Daniel drew up his jumper sleeve and showed me a large, impressive black watch. 'Good to thirty metres underwater,' he said tapping it, 'and there's a stopwatch and an alarm, too.'

Maggie and Diana were down on their knees in the lounge room, both of them filling holes and talking. I was pleased Maggie had wrapped a purple scarf, turban-like, around her head and that she was wearing lipstick, even though she was in the house. It made her look happier, I thought, and Daniel's mum, too, was wearing lipstick, a pale brownish pink colour that seemed to match her hair and her jumper perfectly. Next to Diana's soft colours, Mum's purple scarf and brightly-striped jumper looked almost too bold and it made me wonder if they'd ever really be friends. They looked happy, though, working together, and their voices buzzed along in that calm, friendly way, like when there's art at school and everyone's really into it, making masks, say, or clay figures.

I outlined Daniel's plan quickly to Maggie, explaining about the watch and how we'd be back, that we were just exploring, and Maggie said, 'Sure, sure', and if Diana started to say something about the river, I was out of the room too quickly to know whether she'd been about to say it to me or to my mother.

The Captain's Log, Stardate 150901

I took the new coloniser down to Waterway C. in order to acquaint her with the river fauna. Unfortunately the more elusive of these wasn't present, but we did see River Rodents, known commonly as water rats. I held my breath, actually, in case she thought these were disgusting — other colonisers have — but Rain thought they were pretty cute.

They are, too. They are quite cheeky, have a white tip on the end of their tail and they are frequently mistaken for platypuses, because they share the same environment. I must say, the number of water rats I have seen makes me doubt my original platypus sighting (see Captain's Log, Stardate 220400). It could be that it was rats all the time. It's not that I don't like the rats, and they are, as the Counsellor says, quite special in their own way, but they are not platypuses. This isn't what I told Rain, of course — I said we only had to wait long enough and we'd see a platypus.

I don't think this was wrong of me. I haven't much bargaining power, as the Ferengi would put it, and I need every bit I have. Otherwise she'll get to school and she'll never speak to me again.

I am the most unpopular kid in Clarkson P S and that's that. There is no one worse at sports and better at all other subjects, except for art. There is no one more likely to get tripped up, spat at, head butted, accidentally kicked, pushed and punched, or have their lunch end up in the dust. I spend my lunch time trailing around after the teacher on duty and playing two papers with the loneliest preppies.

I don't imagine Rain will be my friend at school. Or, really, that I even want her to. If she's my friend, they won't let her be anyone else's. And what have I got that they don't have?

What I have	versus	*What they have*
we live next door		cool
her mum and mine are friends		pony club
internet access		scouts
chess games		ballet
platypus (if we see any — otherwise water rats)		boyfriends

It doesn't look good on my side. She'll spend one day at Clarkson P S and be swept up by the tutu and jodphur girls and then Tom will be her boyfriend and she won't even want to learn chess.

Now I am descending into depression, as the Counsellor says.

Rain's First Weekend Away Fridge Poem

this girl
will miss you
my most
& only
my always
a fat kiss
& no sad
from me
your daughter

(Why do they have the word 'father' in this poetry set
but not the word 'mother'. I should write to them and
complain.)

The Captain's Log, Stardate 211001

The next-door colonisers set out early after lunch and the first female came back alone in her transport pod around dusk.

On Planet 9 we ate heartily and then the screen went on and I went to the bridge. All quiet. Read for a while — *The Hobbit* — but the television noise got me down so I opened the blinds and looked out into the night. Well, I should have, but the first female had her blinds open, too, so I saw straight into Planet 7's eating pod.

Honest, I was hoping for stars. And there was Maggie walking up and down the kitchen in her pyjamas already (and not even my bedtime), her face all funny.

I thought she may have had a stroke and nearly called the doctor, but I decided further investigation was necessary so got the star binoculars out and focussed on her.

Her face was all pulled in and she was crying, but her hands were moving as though she was dancing slowly to some music. She didn't bother to sweep the tears away, just kept on swaying and crying.

The Counsellor cries, of course, but she drops her face into her hands and snuffles quietly, and when she lifts her head again she smiles a watery, rivery smile and tells us that she loved that particular patient very much or was thinking of their children or their parents, depending on who has died or who has to be told they have cancer. Dad and I push the teapot over to her or massage her shoulders.

She cries at the television, too, but there's no television in Rain's kitchen.

Maggie could be missing Rain. Rain said she was staying with her dad this weekend.

This must be the first anthropological secret gathered by Planet 9 about Planet 7. The older coloniser cries until tears leave her eyes and spread across her face when the second coloniser leaves to stay with her paternal family.

I suppose that's natural. Would the Counsellor cry over me? Yes. Would the doctor? He'd do his loud throat-clearing noise that means he's very upset.

Should I tell anyone? And is she actually dancing while she's crying, which is what it looked like? Must investigate further.

The Captain's Log, Stardate 221001

Things I don't know about:
what it would be like to live on Mars
how to build a space rocket
how to go back in time
what sex is all about
how to fall in love

The Doctor said this morning that the Thomas girl had come in with a bad cold and it had turned out she was pregnant. Counsellor Diana gasped and said, 'She was going to get engaged.'

'Looks like they'll skip that and get married,' the Doctor said.

It would be pretty weird to go to the doctor for the flu and come out knowing you were going to have a baby.

The Counsellor packed her old people's bag — she's off to deliver her Saturday cake and comfort. And then, as the Doctor has the morning off, they were going to play golf. They invited me but I admit I find golf boring and frustrating.

I went to Maggie's. I wanted to make sure she wasn't still crying. I wanted to see if so much crying left lasting marks.

She looked absolutely normal except she was wearing a weird purple t-shirt and baggy black trousers and her hair was all over the place.

'Rain's at her dad's,' she said when she opened the door.

'I know,' I said. 'I've come over to see how you are.'

'Oh,' she said, 'I'm fine, thank you. Would you like to come in?'

'Thanks,' I said, and sat down at the kitchen table.

'Tea?' she asked. 'Or coffee?'

'I'm too young for coffee,' I said. 'Tea would be lovely, thanks.'

'Raisin toast? I haven't had breakfast yet and was just about to make some.'

'Just one piece, thanks. If it isn't too much trouble.'

'Not at all.'

'Well,' Maggie said, passing me the butter, 'is this an official visit or just a pop-over and how's your morning?'

'Were you dancing last night? When you were crying, I mean?'

'You saw me?'

'I couldn't help it,' I said. 'You hadn't drawn the blinds.'

'We took the blinds down,' Maggie said. 'I don't like blinds. I'm going to make curtains.'

'So were you? Dancing?'

'And crying.' Maggie nodded. 'I miss Rain and I like to cry with music on.'

'She'll be back, though,' I said. 'It's only for the weekend, isn't it?'

'Yes,' Maggie said, 'but it was the first weekend and it's always hard to do new things for the first time, so you have to be a little gentle with yourself and if you feel like crying, you should.'

'I cried the first day of school.'

'There you are then, you know what I mean.'

'I still cry, sometimes. You won't tell Rain, will you?'

'Of course not. Why do you still cry?'

'No one likes me much at school. I can't do the things they like.'

'What things can't you do?'

'Soccer, football and cricket — stuff like that. I can't play contact sports of any kind and I'm not much good at the physical stuff either. I have a cardiac condition.'

'I didn't know that,' Maggie said. 'More toast?'

'Just one more, thanks. It's okay, it doesn't mean I'll have a heart attack or anything like that.'

'Right,' Maggie said. 'So do the other kids know that?'

'I suppose so.'

'Have you told Rain?'

'Do I have to?'

'It's up to you.'

'I thought if she knew she might — she might think she had to be my friend because she felt sorry for me.'

'I see,' Maggie said, 'On the other hand, if she finds out from someone else, she might feel hurt that you didn't tell her yourself.'

'I guess I'll tell her later, okay?'

I like Maggie. I like the fact that she didn't make too big a deal of my heart stuff or the fact that I'm unpopular at school. Even if she does stay up half the night crazily dancing and crying, she's a really calm person. It's like she's deeply calm. Whereas the Counsellor, who you'd think would be calm, just isn't. I can't tell *her* how unpopular I am. She'd just worry and worry.

Aren't people odd? I wonder if I'll be as strange when I grow up?

City Weekend

You would think there'd be more to do in the city than the country, but I missed the Dreamhouse and Mum all weekend. Maybe it was because Maggie and I are fixing up the house and maybe because everything's new there. Dad picked me up at Sunbury Maccas, but because he'd left work early to do that he had to work most of Saturday, so Julia and I spent the day together.

If I had to write an essay on what I did on the weekend I could do it in one word — SHOP! We started at the market, which was okay except that Julia had a list so she didn't browse around the way Maggie and I used to. If you have a list you just go bang, bang down the list and don't even stop for a coffee or a jam donut. Then you load the stuff in the car and walk down to a café where you sit for hours, much longer than it's taken you to do the shopping, drink two coffees and read the paper and there's nothing, absolutely nothing to look at except all the other café sitters. Julia wouldn't even play that game where you pick a person and imagine a life for them. She said, 'No, Rain, please, I'm trying to read the paper', in a tone that made me wonder if I had given her a hard time over anything.

I hadn't. I hadn't complained when Dad went to work. I'd washed the breakfast dishes — not that she knew that, because she was still in bed when Dad and I had breakfast. I'd sat really quietly until she was ready to go out and I hadn't even asked if I could have the television on because I know she doesn't like it on first thing in the morning, although by then it was about nine thirty. All I had done was try to shop the way Maggie and I do.

'Oh look,' I said, 'fresh pasta, Julia — that would be good for dinner.'

'We're going out for dinner,' she said. 'I don't cook on the weekends if I can avoid it. A new Thai restaurant's opened up.'

'There's a Thai restaurant in Clarkson,' I said. 'Mum reckons that puts it on the map.'

'I think it would take more than a Thai restaurant to put Clarkson on the map, Rain,' Julia said with a little laugh. 'Still, if your mum's happy there.'

'We're both very happy there,' I said.

You'd think you'd have a great big lunch after you'd been to the market, wouldn't you? Maggie and I would put packets of cheese, little containers of sundried tomatoes, olives, artichoke hearts, sometimes pickled octopus, ham or terrine and two loaves of bread on the table and we'd sit down to a feast. Dad would sit there rubbing his hands together.

Julia found some peanut butter scrapings in the cupboard, a few pale cherry tomatoes and some left-over pesto.

'I'm not very domesticated,' she said. 'Sorry, Rain. Your father and I don't eat at home much. You just tell me what you want in future and I'll try to make sure I have it. Are you sure you don't want some yoghurt? We seem to have plenty of that.'

I ate bread spread thinly with peanut butter while Julia whizzed up her beetroots and yoghurt into a pale pink drink which looked beautiful but smelt earthy.

'Well,' she said when we'd finished, 'up for some shopping?'

We mooched along Chapel Street where Julia tried on five dresses, three tops, three skirts, a pair of trousers and two coats. Not all at the same shop, of course. We went to nine different boutiques. She put a coat on lay-by — it was four hundred and fifty dollars, I couldn't help hearing. And it was plain black. You'd expect to get something special for that much money, like a bit of braid or a fluffy collar or something, but this was just black. It looked to me exactly like the coat she was wearing, but the sales assistant and Julia raised their eyebrows at each other and twittered together when I said that. And then Julia said, and I don't think she thought I'd hear her but I did, 'She's my stepdaughter, from the country.'

And that's when I decided I hated her. She had no right to call me her stepdaughter when she and Dad weren't even married, and anyway, no one had asked me whether I wanted to be called that. I would certainly never in a million trillion years have called Julia my stepmother and I wasn't going to start, thank you very much. Little kids might have stepmothers, but not Rain May Carr-Davies. It made it sound as though Maggie had died. It was awful.

At the next shop she tried on a little jumper with lots of different coloured stripes.

'Too young, do you think?' she asked the mirror.

'Those colours are very popular,' I said and the sales assistant beamed at me. 'All the teenagers where I live are wearing them.' Then, remembering what Mum and Fran said to each other whenever they went shopping, I said, 'I think you'd get away with it, Julia. After all, you're still pretty young, aren't you? I mean, Dad's years older than you, isn't he?'

She didn't buy it, of course. Which was a shame, really, because I had to admit it had suited her. But I didn't care. By the time we got back to the flat, we were both grumpy and tired. Dad was cross, too.

'I got home early so I could go out with my girls,' he said, 'and the flat was empty. Where have you been?'

'Just buying a few things,' Julia said. 'Oh darling, I'm sorry you came home to a lonely old flat. Shall we have a spa together? I'm just exhausted and I'm sure you are, too. Rain can watch television.'

'Fine with me,' I said, 'Is there anything to eat? I'm starving.'

'Oh heavens, I don't think we have any snacks,' Julia said. 'Not very good for you, particularly after a big lunch.'

'It wasn't a big lunch,' I said. 'There's nothing to eat here, Dad. I had ancient peanut butter for lunch, I've been dragged from clothes shop to clothes shop all day and I'm hungry.' I didn't mean my voice to go up in a wail but it did and I felt perilously close to crying.

'You run the spa bath, Julia darling. Rain and I will go out and have a quick snack. I'm a little hungry, too.'

'Don't be long then. And don't eat anything silly, darling. Remember that cholesterol.'

We had baclavas at a Turkish café nearby.

'I'm sorry you two aren't getting on well,' he said, stirring a heaped spoonful of sugar in his short black. 'I thought you liked Julia.'

I shrugged. 'She's okay,' I said, 'it's just the shopping. And she called me her stepdaughter. Which I'm not. And it sounded as though Maggie had died.'

'That's a bit extreme, Rain. She was probably just trying to explain the relationship.'

'Get real, Dad. To a sales assistant? As if it mattered?'

Dad reached across the table and took my hand.

'Give her some time, please,' he said. 'She's not used to kids. She's a lovely person, Rain, honestly. She'll learn how to cope. We'll just have to teach her slowly. Okay, just for me?'

'You haven't even asked how Maggie is,' I said. 'You haven't asked after her at all. I want to ring her. I want to ring her when we get back. When you two are relaxing in your spa, I want to ring my mother.'

'That's fine. Of course you can ring her, Rain. But I don't like this attitude. Of course I am concerned about your mother, but I can't make you the go-between to find out about her. This is grown-up stuff, Rain. You don't understand all of it.'

'I'm sorry,' I said, and I was, even though I might not have sounded it. Dad knew I was, because he held my hand again and asked me just to try while they got this new situation sorted out and everyone was more used to everything and each other.

'Tomorrow,' he said, 'will be our day. We'll do something together, just the two of us, okay?'

I did ring Maggie but I didn't tell her how miserable I was. I said everything was okay and I was okay, just missing her a little bit, and how was she and had she read the poem on the fridge I'd left her? And she said she loved me and that she missed me and, yes, it was a wonderful poem and thank you very much and that Daniel had joined her for breakfast and they'd had raisin toast. When I hung up I felt kind of better on the one hand and slightly more miserable on the other.

I had thought that the weekend would be fantastic. I thought I'd drop enough hints about the Dreamhouse and the platypus and the mist in the mornings that Dad would want to come up and see it all.

Well, I tried. I talked about the Dreamhouse over dinner at the Thai restaurant, where we had to take our shoes off at the door and sit nearly on the floor on these big cushions, which was fun. Every time I mentioned something that we were doing, Julia talked about the food. She wasn't even interested in the possum, although Dad loved hearing that story.

'How sweet,' he said. 'So are they living in the possum house?'

'We think so,' I said. 'The food we put out disappears, which Mum says is a good sign.'

'Did you hear that, Julia, the possums moved in to the house.'

'Yes, that's lovely. Now, what are your plans for tomorrow?'

Really, the best thing I did all weekend was email my friend Emma in Sydney and tell her all about everything. Of course she knew Maggie and Dad were splitting up — that had started to happen before she left Melbourne, but she didn't know Mum and I had moved to the country, or that my bedroom was purple or about Daniel. So I had lots to tell her.

'Daniel is this really cool boy,' I wrote to Em. 'He's terribly smart and quite good-looking and knows all about all sorts of things. He's really into Star Trek and chess and computers.' That made him sound too nerdy.

'He's good at basketball, too,' I lied, 'and horse riding and he's nearly two years older than me and all the girls in Clarkson really like him so its pretty good luck that I ended up next door.' That sounded okay, so I thought I'd give Julia a make-over as well.

'The flat where Julia and Dad are living is practically a mansion,' I wrote. 'I have this huge room with a balcony and my own private bathroom.' Actually my room was the size of a cupboard and I had to use Julia and Dad's bathroom, which I think annoyed Julia, although she cleared me a space in the cupboard for my toothbrush and anything else I needed to put there.

'Julia's great,' I wrote. 'We went shopping together today and she bought me a new denim skirt and one of those striped ribbed jumpers everyone in Melbourne is wearing this winter.'

Sunday was Dad's and my day and I chose the zoo because it was a bright winter morning and I knew the animals would be out and busy in the cooler weather.

'The zoo,' Julia said. 'Oh can I come, too? I love the zoo.'

'Well, it was to be my day with Rain,' Dad said, looking at me, 'but I don't see why you couldn't come, do you, Rain?'

Actually I could think of a long list of reasons, but Julia said please very nicely and she even laughed when I said, 'Well, only if you're good', and no one told me off for being cheeky so I thought maybe she'd just needed a good sleep.

And it was a great day. I was right about the animals — they were all out and about, even the ones you don't often see. The big bears looked happy for once. We'd seen them in summer and they'd looked really miserable wearing such heavy fur coats.

In the late afternoon Dad and I left the flat to drive back to Sunbury. He rang Maggie from his mobile and said that he might as well drive me all the way home, if that didn't interfere with her plans, because it meant that he and I could have a good talk. And I was delighted because he'd see the Dreamhouse and know that everything else was a big mistake.

I finally got to tell him everything — all the stuff I hadn't felt comfortable saying in front of Julia. I told him about Daniel and the platypus and how odd he is but I like him anyway. And how Diana is so vague and pretty but has this carpenter's apron, and aren't people funny, never quite who you think they are. And it was as though he hadn't ever started to work later and later hours, met Julia and then moved out entirely.

When we pulled up at the house Dad said, 'Right, out you get, squirrel. Don't forget your bag.' And I realised that he wasn't even going to get out of the car, not even to come inside to look at my bedroom, let alone sit down and have a cup of tea with Maggie.

'Aren't you going to come in?' I said.

'No, love, no, I can't. Your mother wouldn't like it, and anyway I have to get back or Julia will be furious. We're seeing a show tonight, don't want to be late.'

'But Dad — okay, I'll get my bag.'

'Kiss?' he asked and I unbuckled my seat belt and leant across and kissed him.

'I'm sorry squirrel, I know it's hard. Look, I'll ring you, okay? I've got some ideas for the next weekend. And I was thinking of getting a Playstation, for weekends when we didn't want to do anything. What do you think?'

'That'd be great, Dad.'

'I thought you really wanted one.'

'Yeah. Sort of.'

'Look, Rain, I'm trying here.'

'It'd be great, Dad, okay?'

'And if you're into *Star Trek* now, I know someone with the biggest collection of videos in the world, a real expert in the field.'

'I'm not into *Star Trek*, Dad. That's Daniel.'

'I love you,' he called out, but I had my bag and was heading for the front door. I didn't even turn around to wave.

Maggie opened the door for me so quickly it was as though she'd been waiting behind it.

'You could have come out and said hello,' I said.

'Well, I didn't,' Maggie said and hugged me. 'Hey, I missed you.'

'I missed you, too,' I said, 'and I'm starving.'

'Soup?' Maggie asked. 'Maggie's super duper minestrone? With garlic bread?'

'Oh Mum.' I hugged her, squeezing myself against her so she had to hold me hard or fall over. 'I love your soup, I love this house and I specially really love you, a lot.'

'I love you too, Rain. It will get easier, darling, you know that. Remember how you hated school camp the first year and thought you'd never go again? Remember how you cried on your first sleep-over and Em's poor mother had to bring you home at midnight?'

'It's not that,' I said. 'It's just good being back, you know. The weekend was okay but it's great to be home again.'

Maggie's soup was garlicky and full of beans and we ate it in front of the fire in the back room while we looked through the Spotlight catalogue for curtain material. We told each other about our weekend, but

I didn't tell her about Julia's four hundred and fifty dollar coat or about me putting her off buying a striped jumper and a denim skirt. And I didn't tell her about Julia and Dad having a spa bath together.

I told her instead about the market and how it had made me think about shopping with her, and she said maybe we'd try to get down every so often and stock up on exotic food. I told her about the shops and how there was absolutely nothing in them, and she said she'd have to drag out her old sewing machine and teach me to sew. I told her I liked Thai food and we should go out to our Thai restaurant sometime, to celebrate something, and she looked pleased. And finally I told her about the zoo, the happy bears, the little meerkats with their quick dodging heads and the shambling orangutans.

And then, because it was cold and we'd missed each other, we snuggled up in Maggie's big bed and read to each other from Maggie's special book of fairy tales, where all the princesses make friends with the dragons and ride off on their golden backs so they can find new lands to conquer, in a kindly way, leaving the princes at home with the washing-up and the babies.

'Which is a little silly,' Maggie said, 'because although I wouldn't mind a dragon ride, I wouldn't want to leave my baby behind.'

'Why can't they do both?' I asked. 'Why couldn't they take the baby on the dragon?'

'Maybe they do,' Maggie said. 'When they've made sure the new lands are suitable for babies, maybe then they whizz home quickly, kiss the prince goodbye and grab the babies.'

'Why can't the prince go, too? Why can't they ring the prince from the new land and the prince packs up the babies, grabs another dragon and flies off to join the princess?'

'Because the prince was scared of dragons,' Maggie said. 'Remember?'

'If I wrote it,' I said, 'I'd put a plane in. That's what I'd do. The prince could follow her with the babies in a plane. They'd land and she'd meet them at the airport in a taxi and they'd live happily ever after.'

Home Again Rain

celebrate
cake
pie
champagne
she is home
my melon baby
wild green girl
my other heart
my daughter

The Captain's Log, Stardate 011001

First day back at the Training Academy. I warned Lieutenant Rain not to associate too closely with me. She didn't listen.

'They'll get you,' I said. 'They'll get you because they hate me.'

'You're my friend, Daniel,' she said, 'I'm with you.'

Old Khan put Rain at my table. Which is the last place you'd want to sit if you had a choice. The best table, the star table, is Tom's. He's an average student but good at everything else. He, Oliver, Michael and Craig aren't rocket scientists by any means, but out in the playground they're officer material and you'd better not forget it. Head of the girls is Tom's twin, Becky. They're not identical. She's bright but pretends not to be. That gets me with girls. Why do they do that?

Even the Counsellor — a dab hand at cupboards and fixing things — gets in a flap about filing. Why can't she just say, I'm great at making cupboards and putting up tree-houses? That's what they always tell me to do. Concentrate on your best assets, she and the Doctor say, not on what you can't do. In my case this means everything other than thinking.

Rain should have been put with Becky. They'd probably get on.

Did Khan think he was doing Rain a favour putting her on the losers table? I think he actually thought he was.

'Rain,' he said. 'Rain, what an interesting name.'

'I'm named after a poem,' Rain said, 'by e e cummings. Have you ever heard of him?'

'Yes, yes I have. An American poet.'

'He didn't use punctuation or capital letters in his work,' Rain said, 'and people thought he was strange.'

'You must bring in a poem of his one day,' old Khan said. 'I can see why you and Daniel have become friends.'

At snack time Becky said, 'Well, there go the Double Drips.'

The minute I heard it, I knew it would stick. The Double Drips. Very funny, ha ha.

'So what do you do at snack time?' Rain said to me, turning her back on Becky and the rest of the girls.

'It's not too late,' I said. 'You could just kind of walk over, talk about the city, a clothes shop or something. They'd be friends with you.'

'I don't want to,' Rain said. 'I think they're horrible.'

Kids made dripping noises at us all day. When we walked home, even the preppies had caught on. A couple plipped and plopped behind us nearly all the way home.

'Want to do something?' I asked her. 'Do you want to have a game of chess?'

'No thanks, Daniel,' Rain said. 'I think I'll just do my homework, watch some television. I'm feeling a little down.'

'They'll get over it,' I said. 'You'll become part of the furniture.'

'See you tomorrow,' she said and gave the smallest wave.

The Doctor was called out just before dinner — a bad fall. So the Counsellor and I ate dinner together and I asked her what she'd do if she felt she had caused someone to get an undeserved reputation.

'Just as a matter of curiosity,' I said.

'Well,' she said, 'I wouldn't like myself much if I stood by and let someone be put in prison for something they didn't do.'

It's funny how she automatically goes for the worst thing you could think of.

'Not like that,' I said. 'Suppose that by, I don't know, being someone's friend, you caused them not to be liked by other people.' That was a little too close to the truth but I kept my fingers crossed.

'That's an interesting question,' the Counsellor said. 'People do get judged by their associates, don't they? And to some extent, it's fair enough. People with common interests tend to gather together.'

She went on and on. That's the problem with asking adults anything — they ramble on and never get to the point. Hours later I finally got to read *Lord of the Rings*. Dad wants me to finish it before I see the film. I'm going to learn Elvish when I finish it. I think that could be very useful for secret messages.

The Captain's Log, Stardate 021001

Stormy weather, alien interference.

I hate fourth term. The star table stole my hat at snack time and wouldn't give it back. Rain marched up and demanded they hand it over. The result was predictable. They wouldn't.

Rain got angrier and angrier and went to grab the hat. Tom held the hat behind his back and when Rain tried to grab it he pushed her. She pushed him back and then suddenly they were scrabbling about in the grass, kicking and shouting.

We all had to see the Principal. Rain and Tom were called in separately. Then I went in as one of the eye-witnesses and the chief cause. I told Mrs Crisp as clearly and concisely as I could what had happened.

'Do you feel you are a victim of playground bullying?' Burnt Toast asked.

'Well, not in this instant,' I said. 'It was Rain who was the victim.'

It's the hat, of course. I know the school's policy is for wide-brimmed hats but only preppies, girls and Daniel Gill wears one. The boys wear caps. They get into trouble for it every day but that doesn't stop them. A hat, even one bought from the surf shop, which is where the Counsellor bought mine, isn't cool.

'I hate school,' Rain said, kicking stones all the way home. 'I hate it. It's vile.'

'Are you going to tell Maggie?'

'You bet! She might be able to think of something. Don't you tell the Counsellor?'

'She'd worry,' I said. 'Anyway, nothing changes. I'm just who I am, that's it and they don't like it.'

'I think you're being stupid,' Rain said. 'But that's your business.'

I meant to tell her how sorry I was that she'd got herself into all this just because of my dumb hat, but she ran off into the house before I had the chance.

The Captain's Log, Stardate 041001

Things are worse. Someone wrote Daniel ♥ Rain on the whiteboard. Rain said she didn't care.

'I will not have this silly girlfriend boyfriend stuff in my class, do you hear?' old Khan said, glaring straight at me as though I'd write something like that up for everyone to see.

I don't feel so well. I think this term's got to me already.

Drips, Bullies and
Mr Beatty's Platypus

'School stinks,' I told Maggie, 'and this school stinks most of all.'

Maggie was sitting cross-legged on the floor, her palms resting on her knees. She was looking up at the ceiling but her eyes were closed. She had found a yoga class. I banged my bag on the floor and she hardly winced.

'Daniel and I are victims,' I said. 'Honest, Mum.'

Her eyes opened and she lowered her head.

'Oh Rain, don't exaggerate.'

'I'm not, Mum — I mean Maggie. I'm not exaggerating. This boy-thing took Daniel's hat today and when I tried to get it back, he pushed me over.'

'Really?'

'We all had to go to the Principal's office and she's an old cow. Boy-thing doesn't know his own strength, she implied, because he's so good at sports. Probably didn't mean to push me right over. Tut-tut-tutted at him and that's all. Dismissed. Except for hoping that I will fit in, difficult she knows, but if I make an effort … Mum, are you listening?'

Maggie sighed and stretched out her legs.

'Why did he take Daniel's hat?'

'Because it's his. I don't know. I told you it would be beastly and it is.'

'Bit early to tell that, isn't it?' Maggie didn't sound certain.

'Poor Daniel,' I said. 'He's had this all his life. Imagine. And he's really clever.'

'Do you want me to speak to someone,' Maggie asked slowly, 'or do you want my advice?'

'You can't speak to anyone,' I said. 'Daniel won't tell his mum anything. She worries, he says. Isn't that what mums are supposed to do?'

Maggie laughed. 'Probably. Okay — my advice is to just ignore it, and if you can't ignore it, to tell a teacher, gently though, Rain, without your righteous indignation. Other than that, avoid these kids, okay?'

'Yeah, I knew you'd say that. I say we wage war on them. Daniel and me against the boy-things!'

'That'll just get you into trouble, Rain, and it could get Daniel into trouble, too.'

'It beats me why he didn't try to get his own hat back,' I said.

'He's probably too sensible, Rain.'

'Or he's been beaten up before,' I said gloomily.

Things didn't improve. Practically every day there was some kind of hat incident. Daniel's patience bugged me. All he would do was ask for it back, or, if they made jokes about it, walk away. It irked me. But I was his friend, so I followed.

'What did you do before I came?' I asked him. 'Who did you hang out with?'

'I used to read,' Daniel said. 'I'm not allowed to run around much anyway.'

'Not allowed to? Why?'

He shrugged. 'It's just a thing,' he said.

'Asthma?'

'Just a thing, okay.'

'The Counsellor certainly is a worrier,' I said to Maggie. 'Daniel's not allowed to run around. What kind of a rule is that?'

'Maybe there's a good reason,' Maggie said. She was making bread in the kitchen, pounding the dough on an old butcher's block she'd bought at a clearing sale. I had a turn kneading. It was hard work.

'I reckon she's over-protective, ' I said, 'because it isn't even asthma. Maybe he was born too early and never quite caught up growing. Or maybe his brain took up too much growing energy. He's not even that small, but maybe he was and she hasn't got over worrying.'

'Maybe.'

In the city I had done a lot of things other than school. I had Little Athletics every Saturday, swimming lessons after school on Friday, jazz and tap dancing on Monday nights and creative dance on Tuesdays. During the Christmas holidays I had done a course of circus skills because Maggie said that was better than gymnastics and clay modelling. Some weekends there were festivals on at various places — my favourite was the Chinese New Year, but we had also been to the Vietnamese moon festival, the Spanish fiesta and the Brunswick Music Festival. It seemed as if we were always doing something.

In Clarkson there was nothing. Which was really interesting. I'd get home from school and some days Maggie and I would go for a walk, or I'd join her in her yoga practice. Sometimes we'd muddle around in the garden where Maggie was putting down a no-dig vegie garden. Or I'd go next door and play a game of chess with Daniel or we'd head together down to the river, platypus hunting. On my Maggie weekends, Maggie and I would drive to the Halffields market where we bought vegies. It wasn't as good as the Victoria Market, but Maggie promised that in the school holidays we'd go back there.

'I think we need a dog,' I said. 'I think if you live in the country you really do need a dog.'

'That's not a bad idea,' Maggie said, 'but not a huge one. We want something small and manageable.'

'A happy dog,' I said. 'You know, one of those ones that look as if they are smiling?'

'I'd love a dog,' Daniel said mournfully when I told him we were getting one.

'Well, you could have one, couldn't you?'

'I don't know. The Counsellor isn't that keen on pets. She says they die.'

'Your mum's weird. She's neurotic, that's what she is.' Neurotic was my new word. I'd heard Dad call Julia that on one of my South Yarra weekends. I'd taken them down some beautiful Clarkson tank water and Julia had insisted on boiling it before she'd even have a sip.

The Clarkson Scout Group had a recruitment drive and Maggie talked me into going along.

'I think it sounds daggy,' I said. 'And isn't it just boys?'

'No, there are girl scouts,' Maggie said, 'and camps. It would be something entirely new, Rain. You'd get to do all sorts of interesting things.'

'All the kids from school will be there,' I said, 'and they won't talk to me.'

'There'll be other kids,' Maggie said. 'I asked and kids come from all over because Clarkson has a scout hall and not everywhere else does.'

'I don't want to go doing too much,' I said. 'Not like I was when we lived in the city.'

I enjoyed Scouts, though. Okay, the uniform *was*

daggy and I wasn't too keen on the flag-raising stuff, but the activities were great and there were four other girls — three of whom I didn't know and Becky.

'You should come along,' I said to Daniel, 'you really should. Some of the stuff we do, you'd love. Honest.'

'I don't want to,' Daniel said. 'I'm not into those really physical things.'

'It's not like that. I mean, there's some stuff that is, but you wouldn't have to do it if you didn't want to, I'm sure. Are you all right? You don't want to do anything these days.'

That wasn't quite true. Daniel and I had gone with Maggie to choose a puppy. Mum's yoga friend's dog had pups and we saw them when they were only one week old. We'd chosen a little sandy-coloured girl with a white star on her chest. We weren't going to get her until she was eight weeks old. Daniel had been impressed with the pups and had started an active dog campaign on the Counsellor who showed some vague signs of weakening.

But the best thing Daniel and I did together was go platypus sighting. We went every afternoon for a week before we saw one. We never would have seen one if it hadn't been for Daniel's dad who got word from a patient that a platypus burrow had been found on his land, down near the river. Old Mr Beatty gave Daniel and his dad special permission to trespass on his land.

Daniel was a favourite with his father's patients, particularly the ones who played chess. It beats me why kids who are liked by adults are always the ones not liked at school. Anyway, Daniel, his dad and I went down to the river, all wrapped up in woolly jackets, hats and scarves because even though the weather was getting warmer the evenings were still cold. We sat on the bank of the river, near where the burrow was, and waited. Daniel's dad had brought a thermos of hot chocolate and we shared that really quietly. You couldn't talk, of course — or only in the quietest of whispers — and we tried not to even wriggle. Daniel was really good at being quiet. I kept finding bits of me that itched — my nose would start, and I'd have to scratch it. Then an old mosquito bite would start irritating my knee or my toes would get itchy and I'd long to take off my boots and wriggle them.

We didn't see anything except water rats. I liked the water rats. They swam really well and didn't look rat-like at all, more like little otters from the zoo. They had white tips on their tails and that's what you looked for to make sure that they weren't platypuses, that and their little ears, close to the head but ears nonetheless, whereas you can't see a platypus's ears. Once you saw them on a bank or a log you could easily tell they were rats by the way they loped along, just like otters.

While they were in the water, though, they swam around just like a platypus. You'd be sitting, me trying not to scratch, and suddenly you'd see a moving arrow of water, mostly quite near the bank. You'd hold your breath, waiting, and then the tail would appear with that little white tip and we'd all breathe out at once and pass the thermos around again.

Then, on the fifth afternoon, when I think even Daniel's dad was getting a little impatient, we definitely saw a platypus. It came right under where we were. We'd changed where we sat, gone downstream a bit to a kind of fishing platform that old Mr Beatty had built on the river bank. And there was the arrow of water from where we had been sitting and it moved along the river bank while we held our breaths. The platform we were standing on was right near some bullrushes and we watched the ripples and bubbles and then it came in really close to the shallow water right near where we were. I know I squeaked, because Daniel elbowed me gently. We all peered down and we could just see the flat tail. No white tip. And then it moved into a patch of late sunshine and we saw it more clearly nosing around and then it must have heard something and with a little flip completely disappeared into deeper, shadowed water.

'Well,' Daniel's dad said after a long silence, 'we've seen it, kids.'

'Are you sure it was really a platypus?' Daniel asked. 'If only we'd had a really good look.'

'It was a platypus,' Daniel's dad said firmly. 'Definitely

a platypus. No white tip. No ears. And shy. A rat would have just come up for a second look at us.'

'Wow, we've seen it, Daniel, we've seen it!'

'I can't believe it,' Daniel said. 'I just can't believe it. It all happened too fast.'

'I know what you mean,' his father said, putting an arm around him, 'but the more time you spend watching wild things, the more practised you get at seeing them, so eventually your eye adapts to their speed. But it was, it was truly a platypus. You've joined an exclusive club, kids. Not many people these days have seen a platypus in the wild. Let's go up and tell Mr Beatty, shall we?'

While the Doctor had a drink with Mr Beatty, Daniel and I went over how we'd seen it.

'We could go on safaris,' I said. 'Not the shooting ones, of course — but to see other animals. I'd like to see an echidna, Daniel. You said you'd seen one.'

'Dad and I did. And it saw us and dug down really quickly. But before it could disappear, Dad grabbed it and flipped it over. They've got these great claws, Rain — they're pretty amazing.'

Mr Beatty made us tomato soup from the can, which tasted delicious, and we dunked thick white bread into it. Then he let us toast marshmallows in his fireplace and we took it in turns to hold the toasting fork. The marshmallows were best when the tops went quite brown and the whole thing threatened to wobble off the fork and fall straight into the fire so you had to open your mouth quickly and almost burn it to catch the marshmallow. Then Mr Beatty and Daniel played a game of chess while the Doctor beat me at dominoes.

Mr Beatty had this ancient fluffy cat who sat on my lap the whole time purring. He didn't even move when I leaned forward to toast the marshmallows. And the house, which was tiny, smelt faintly of old toast and woodsmoke and there were photos on the wall of Mrs Beatty who had died years before. When Mr Beatty saw me looking at them he brought out a photo album with all sorts of old photos in it, old cars and ladies in big hats and little boys in sailor suits.

When we left, Mr Beatty gave me a little china statue of a girl. He said she reminded him of me, even though she was wearing a dress and her hair was all neat curls. He gave Daniel a book on astronomy.

'Got to start off-loading stuff,' he said. 'I'll be eighty-eight next year. Even the Doc here doesn't think I'll last forever.'

'You've still a good few years left in you,' Daniel's dad said as they shook hands at the door.

'Ah, it's that spring water. Best thing for a man, eh?' And Mr Beatty winked at us.

'This has been one of the best nights of my life,' I whispered to Daniel as we drove back home. 'I'll remember it forever, won't you?' I had the china statue in my lap. The girl's hair felt smooth under my fingers, and even though it was dark I knew her dress was pale blue, a blue Mr Beatty called duck-egg.

'Yes,' Daniel said, 'I will. First the platypus and it's the first time I've ever come close to beating Mr Beatty at chess.'

'See,' I said, 'you've got friends. You've got heaps of friends, if you think about it. They just aren't the kind of friends most kids have.'

And that was true. Daniel got emails from kids around the world who, like him, were Trekkies. Every two months he went down to Melbourne to meet with other Trekkies at some club. He got stuff in the ordinary mail practically every day — newsletters and magazines that he brought to school and read during free time. He even wrote for some of them.

But none of that made him any friends at school. And sometimes I wondered whether he even wanted ordinary friends. He wouldn't come along to Scouts. He wouldn't come and learn tennis with me. He just didn't try.

'It's no use,' he said when I asked why he didn't, 'it's just no use, Rain. You don't understand. You're new here.' And he got this really stubborn look which meant the conversation was closed, just like that.

Still, it was hard for me. Becky and I were good friends at Scouts and she started to talk to me at school. We liked some of the same things. She was reading some of the same books I was reading, books Daniel claimed were too girly. We both liked basketball. We liked the same music and we both liked to dress up and dance as though we were pop stars, but not so serious.

'Isn't there anyone you used to play with before I came to the school?' I asked Daniel one lunchtime. The girls were playing basketball and I was itching to join them.

'No,' Daniel said, 'but that doesn't mean you have to sit with me if you don't want to. I can read.'

'No, it's fine.' I said.

I watched Tina miss three easy baskets in a row. I could practically feel the ball between my hands and the easy lift of it through the air.

'How are you going, D1 and D2?' Tom, Becky's twin, asked as he went past. It didn't sound unfriendly.

'Pretty good,' I said.

Daniel ignored him.

'How's it going, Dan my man?' Tom asked, standing right in front of Daniel.

'I'm Daniel,' Daniel said, 'and I'm not your man under any circumstances.'

And he stalked off.

'I was only saying hello,' Tom said. 'What's got into your boyfriend?'

'He's not my boyfriend,' I said. 'But I suppose it's hard to tell when someone's being friendly when they've called you names, taken your hat and generally made your life a misery.'

'Come on, we're just kidding. Anyway, why is he so full of himself? Everyone's got a nickname. You don't mind.'

'I don't *like* it,' I said.

'He doesn't want friends,' Tom said, 'otherwise he'd make more of an effort. He's a snob.'

'He's not, that's not true at all.'

'Oh yeah? Well, how come I can't understand half of what he says?'

'He's different,' I said. 'Look, he doesn't mean to talk so you can't understand him. He just uses big words. He reads all the time. It rubs off on him.'

'And if you do something he wants to do — like play chess — it's not like a normal game. He tells you all this stuff.'

'Just like you do when you're playing soccer or something. There's no difference. You tell kids what they should have done, don't you?'

'That's called coaching.'

'Well, Daniel's coaching you at chess. I don't see the difference.'

'I just don't get why you hang out with him. You're pretty cool, Rain, for a city girl.'

'See — there you go again. Always picking on differences.'

'Hey, I just said you were cool.'

'Well, anyway, Daniel's my friend. And he's cool, too.'

'If you say so,' Tom said. 'So you'll be going to the disco with him?'

Fourth-term disco was the highlight of the school year. There were door prizes, best-costume prizes, a smoke machine and a limbo dance.

'I'm not sure I'm going,' I said. 'It could be my dad's weekend.'

'That's right, you're parents are divorced, aren't they? Our cousin from America is coming over here while her parents fight it out. She'll be at the disco.'

'My parents are separated,' I said, 'not really divorced.'

'Right,' Tom said. 'Well, hope they never get divorced. From what Madison says in her emails it's really ugly.'

I found Daniel over near the old play equipment. He looked all pale and blotchy, but when I asked he just said he wasn't feeling well, and halfway through individual project time he stood up and said in a shaky voice that he felt sick.

And I didn't see him for the rest of the week.

'Gastro,' Diana said, when I rang to find out how he was.

And then the next day she said something about a virus.

I played basketball every lunchtime, and every

snack time I talked about the disco with the girls. But even though I loved the magic feeling when the ball sails perfectly through the hoop or when you bounce it away from the other team, and even though I wanted to go to the disco more than anything else in the world, I still missed Daniel. It was as though there was a piece of the school day that was missing and nothing felt quite right.

Rain's Basketball Poem

fly from my hand
like magic
a breeze
and sail
up & over
bounce down
hard
such splendid
joy.

Maggie's Yoga Poem

breath
in
out
belly soft
learn slow
I am only
me
peace.
Then go & eat
cake
more delicious than ever!

The Captain's Log, Stardate 271001

Sick of being sick. Gastro, the Counsellor said. Dry crackers and lemonade prescribed. Then I felt fine and so she let me eat. Then I threw up — but I didn't feel sick, not like gastro. I just felt — I don't know — tired.

Too tired to do much at all. Don't even want to be writing this but I know I should.

Too tired to play chess so the Doctor and I play backgammon instead. I'm current world champion but I don't really care. It's mainly luck.

Diana measured me yesterday and I've really grown since last time.

She looked worried.

'I'm supposed to grow,' I said but she ignored me.

Interesting fact: Rain has called every night.

Interesting fact number two: my ankles seem bigger. Do your ankles grow thicker? That's pretty strange. But they do, they seem bigger. Not that I pay much attention to my ankles. It was just that there was a scab I had to pick.

Hearts and Hurts

Every morning I waited for Daniel to arrive at the front door to pick me up on his way to school. And every morning, Diana came out and shook her head.

'Not really well yet,' she'd call out to me, 'but getting better. If you could pick up any work he's missing, I'd be grateful, Rain.'

Daniel wasn't missing any work. He was so far ahead of the rest of us it was a laugh. What he was missing was all the talk of the disco and of Tom and Becky's American cousin who had arrived but was still suffering from jet lag.

'She's got so many clothes,' Becky told us. 'And they're so, I don't know — American.'

'What do you mean, American?'

'Well, like she's got this t-shirt with the American flag on it. And the jeans, they don't look like our jeans. They're American jeans. And the way she talks, too — she really drawls. And everything's like wow and cute.

And if they're not, they're like so yesterday. And she has these opinions about everything.'

'What do you mean? Everyone has opinions.'

'It's like she knows exactly what she wants. And likes. And doesn't like. She's really definite about it. Like someone's mother.'

'She's pretty cool,' Tom said, sauntering up bouncing a basketball. 'She's got like these really American teeth, each one perfect. She wants to meet you, Rain, because you have something in common — with your folks, you know, being separated and everything.'

'Can't wait,' I muttered and walked away, wishing Daniel was there.

I did miss Daniel at school — and I didn't. I mean I did, mostly all the time, but I also liked talking to Becky, playing basketball, just fooling around with the other kids. They still called me D2, but it was in a friendly way. If Daniel had been there and part of it, it would have been great. But it wouldn't have been so great if he'd been there but sulking or miserable.

And I knew the disco would be the same. Even though Daniel had said he was going, I couldn't imagine him going and having fun. I couldn't see Daniel dancing. I couldn't even imagine what he'd wear. And half of me, the mean, nasty half of me, didn't want him to go because I didn't want to have to sit in a corner with him, watching. I wanted to be out there, dancing my socks off and having fun.

It was a problem, all right. It was bigger than me, for sure. I'd have to consult Maggie, but when I got home she started talking before I was even properly in the front door.

'Diana's taken Daniel down to the Royal Children's,' she said. 'I think you should know that he's got cardiac problems, heart problems.'

'What?' I dumped my bag on the floor. 'What are you talking about?'

'Daniel's sick. He's going to need an operation.'

'What heart problems? Like Gran had? Is he going to die?'

'No, sweetheart. Not like Gran. There are problems you can be born with when your heart doesn't function properly. Daniel's heart is like that.'

'He never told me.'

'No. He probably didn't want you to feel sorry for him. Or maybe he was embarrassed.'

'Is he going to die?'

'No, no, of course not. Diana said he's under the best care. They've known this would happen eventually.'

'Poor Daniel,' I said. 'Oh Mum, that's awful. He should have told me. I was kind of mean to him today.'

'How could you have been, he wasn't even at school.'

'Well, I thought mean thoughts, about the school

disco. Oh Mum, I shouldn't have. I wished he'd stay away until it was over. It's all my fault.'

'Rain, don't be so melodramatic. I've just told you, they've all known that this surgery would be necessary one day. It was a case of when, that's all. Daniel's latest growth spurt has put some extra strain on his heart. They're going to correct that. It's got nothing to do with you.'

Maggie was good to cry on. She smelled of bread and incense.

'Rain,' Maggie said gently, 'it's okay. It'll be okay. And you are a good friend. Do stop crying now. There's a girl.'

'Is that why Diana's so over-protective?' I asked at last, all cried out. 'And do you think that's why Daniel doesn't run around much?'

'Yes, yes, I think so.'

'Mum, did you know?'

'Well, yes, Rain, yes I did.'

'Did Diana tell you?'

'No. Daniel told me.'

'Daniel told *you*. He told you and not me?'

'When you were away that first weekend.'

I didn't get it. Why would your best friend tell your mother something that they couldn't tell you?

'He didn't know you very well then,' Maggie said, putting her arm around me. 'He didn't know you at all, really. You weren't friends then like you are now.'

'Well, he could have told me now,' I said, 'and it would have made sense.'

'That's not what is important now,' Maggie said. 'What's important is that we help Daniel and his family.'

'I don't know what to do.'

'Well, it sounds like he might be in hospital for some time. Could you ask Dad to take you in for a visit next weekend?'

'Would that be all right? To visit him?'

'We'll check with Diana, but hospitals usually welcome visitors. Anything that cheers the patients up.'

'I have to go and see a friend in hospital,' I told Dad, 'this weekend. In the Royal Children's Hospital. Daniel — you know, the boy next door?'

'He's in hospital?'

'Heart stuff. He was born with it.'

'Well, we'll ring up the hospital and find out the visiting hours, but I can't guarantee to be able to take you myself. This weekend there's work stuff happening. Now, don't you start, Rain. I've had Julia on my back about it all week. I'm sure she'll take you in, if it's not possible for me.'

'I've work stuff, too,' Julia said. 'I told them I'd be available all weekend. Honestly Brian, you're not the only one working here.'

'Well, you'd only be in at the Royal Children's,' Dad said. 'Wouldn't that be nearly as available as here at the flat?'

'Hardly. I can't access work from the hospital.'

'But if they rang, we could just leave, couldn't we?' I asked.

'I suppose so. It's not terribly convenient.'

In the end she took me in to the hospital, but we left much later than we were supposed to because her work did need her and she was on the computer for ages trying to sort something out. So when we finally got in, the visiting hours were over. The nurse was sorry but all she could do, she said, was let me write a note which she absolutely promised to give Daniel.

I didn't say anything, but when we got back to the flat I packed my bag and waited for Dad to come home. I knew it wasn't all Julia's fault. I knew it wasn't all Dad's fault. But I was sick of them both.

'I want to go home,' I told him when he walked in, 'and I want to go now. Neither of you really want me here. And I don't want to be here.'

'What's wrong, what's happened?'

'We got to the hospital after visiting hours,' I said, 'and I hate her and I hate you, too. I'm going home to Maggie.'

'You can't do that, Rain. I'm sure Julia didn't mean to be late.'

'Just like you didn't mean to work. But you always

do. I'm only here every other weekend but you still have to work. Mum would never do that. Mum cares about people. You and Julia just care about things. And work.' I was nearly crying but I kept my voice cold and hard.

'Rain, you don't understand, you're just a kid. Adult things are complicated.'

'Daniel's just a kid, too. And he's my friend and he might not even know why I haven't come to see him.'

'I'm sorry.'

'I just want to go home to Maggie.' I could feel my voice rising into a shriek and I didn't care. I could feel anger and sadness bubbling through me like gas in a bottle. 'You don't care about me. You don't care about anyone. You and Julia are a good match. I hate you both and I want to go home.' I was shouting now, so all the trendy neighbours in Julia's trendy apartment block would hear me. 'You're a selfish, selfish pig and you don't deserve Mum and me.' I took a deep breath. 'I want to go home and I'm going to scream until you take me.'

'I think you'd better take her home straightaway,' Julia said. 'She's hysterical.'

'I hate you,' I screamed. 'I hate you.'

'I think you'd better take her home now, Brian, and we'd all better have some breathing space. Brian?'

All I said to Dad on the whole drive home was that I would never forgive him, ever, for as long as I lived.

Maggie met us at the door, hugged me and told me to go to my room. She and Dad had to talk, she said. This was the first time Dad had seen our dream home, but I didn't care. I didn't want to live with him ever again. I put a CD in my player and lay down on my bed with my hot eyes closed and let the music beat through my body until I stopped thinking about anything but the rhythm of the music. When I woke up, the music had stopped, Dad had gone home and Mum was in her dressing gown drinking a mug of Sleepy Time tea.

'You were asleep,' she said. 'Dad said goodbye, but you were asleep.'

'I hate him,' I said, 'and I hate Julia.'

'I think your father needs to reorganise his priorities,' Maggie agreed, 'but he loves you, Rain, and he really did think Julia would be able to take you to see Daniel. It's just unfortunate the way it turned out.'

'I'm glad he left us for that ... that bimbo,' I said. 'I'm glad we don't live with him anymore.'

Maggie sighed and drew me close to her. She smelled of sandalwood incense and the little tendrils of her hair were damp from the bath. 'It's an adjustment period,' she said, stroking my forehead. 'In a way, it's sort of good that it happened. I think Dad's realised that he has to fit into your life, too. It's not just a matter of you fitting into his. That's a hard lesson, sweetie. Give him a chance.'

'I'm not going back,' I said. 'I'm never staying there again. I'm never seeing them again. Ever.'

'You're seeing them tomorrow,' Maggie said. 'Your father is driving back, all this way, to pick you up and you are all going to visit Daniel tomorrow. And you are going to be on your best behaviour, Rain, because you said some hurtful things to both of them.'

'They were all true,' I said.

'The truth can be hurtful, sweetheart. More hurtful, often, than when someone tells you lies. Because you know it's true. I think you've shaken them both a bit. But Rain, you must also be big enough to forgive them and give them a second chance. That's the real test, isn't it?'

'I don't know what you mean.'

'The real test of how brave and loving you can be is when you allow someone to make a mistake and you keep loving them, despite that mistake. Now, I'm not going to ask you to apologise for anything you said. But I am going to ask you to be the best person you can be.'

'Why? He left us, Mum. He didn't care enough about us to stay. Why should I be the best person for him?'

'Sweetie, marriages are messy things. Who knows when something starts to go wrong? No one person is to blame. Under different circumstances it could have been someone new coming into my life, not Dad's. I could have been the one who left.'

'You wouldn't have left without me.'

'Of course not, but I might have made you live with the someone I'd met.'

I thought about this. I tried to see Maggie with a mysterious Mr X by her side. I tried to imagine them in Julia's spa bath together. I tried to imagine them kissing, the way I had seen Dad and Julia kissing. It didn't work. I could only see Dad's shadow by her side.

'Do you think you could still meet someone?'

'I'm not completely over the hill yet.' Maggie laughed. 'And I've still got all my hair. You never know.'

'It's not that I think you're over the hill,' I said. 'It's just that you seem, I don't know, somehow complete, just by yourself.'

'Oh Rain.' Maggie hugged me. 'That's just about the best thing you could have said to me!'

I didn't understand why she seemed to be nearly crying, but I decided that Dad and she were right — adults are complicated messy people with complicated messy lives. Then and there I vowed I'd never be like that. My life would be organised. It would be more like Diana's, colour-coordinated, neatly folded and prepared for any emergency.

Poem

I miss the star boy
worry
for him
and his broken heart.

Daughter

life is hard
cloud girl
& sacred
devour it ferociously
the green & the blue
the kiss & the salt
trust good angels
to surround you two
always
& god to bring every child
home

The Captain's Log, Supplemental, Stardate 301001

Sick bay.

Turns out my ankles were getting bigger. They were getting bigger because they were swelling because my heart wasn't working properly. Water retention. Proper name: oedema. A sign of cardiac failure.

Now I'm on medication but they're still going to operate even though my ankles are normal again.

The Counsellor has been here every day from breakfast time, practically, until lights out. The Doctor made her go home early tonight. He said she'd break down if she didn't have one good night's sleep. I'm lonely. I was talking to Phil, one of the nurses, but a new kid just came in, so it's all systems go.

The hospital doesn't sleep, ever. Last night a police helicopter landed — must have picked someone up from a country hospital. We all went to the window and watched them land it, guys with long laser torches. At night the lights go down, but kids whimper and moan, and nurses come around and check you. I woke up the other morning at six and this little toddler was being prepped for an operation.

I'll have to have an operation, but only when my surgeon comes back from overseas.

I'll have to have an operation.

The Doctor says that the statistics are well in my

favour. The Counsellor tells me I have the constitution of an ox. They both tell me I am brave and strong. They both tell me I will come through this with flying colours. They both tell me how much they love me. They both look scared.

I'm scared.

I try not to be. I went on the Intensive Care Unit tour and asked careful questions and nodded at everything that was said, but all I could see were sick children with tubes coming out of them. That's all I could see and that was all the Counsellor could see, I know, because she held my hand very tightly the whole time and I couldn't pull away from her.

It's not so bad when Mum's here. She brought in the *Enterprise* model and we're making it on a little table that's set up near the window. The nurses come and help sometimes. When we're bored we take a break and go down to the canteen and outside to the playground.

The Doctor says we've made my bit of the ward look like home. But even though it is all very interesting being here and I do feel I have learnt a lot, I long to go home, back to my own bed and my own room.

Most of all I miss hearing them talk at night. The darkness and stillness of our country nights. Here there is always noise and bustle, right through the night.

And I miss Rain. She was going to come and see me

today but didn't. She sent me a note instead. It wasn't her fault they didn't make it. It was Julia's fault, the note said.

By the time I get back to school, they'll have taken her. Becky and she are already friends. I watched her the other day. I knew she would rather have been playing basketball with the girls than sitting talking to me.

By the time I get out of here, I'll have lost the one friend I've had in years.

I don't want to write any more. I'm not feeling well.

Aliens Everywhere

Maggie got up early and made her date and chocolate surprise muffins for morning tea. When Julia and Dad arrived, the breakfast dishes were all washed, incense was burning in the lounge room and everything else smelt of muffins. She insisted on taking Julia right through the house, showing her the renovations we had done. Julia admired the paint work and the old dresser the Counsellor and Maggie were stripping and even ate two muffins. If it had been up to me those muffins would have been date and poison, not date and chocolate, surprises.

Dad apologised to me. 'I'm sorry, Rain. Work's been unbelievable lately with this upgrade we're doing, but I promise nothing like that will ever happen again.'

I thought he was going to kiss me and I wasn't ready for that yet, so I scooted backwards and held out my hand instead.

'Peace?' Dad asked taking it.

'Peace,' I said and we shook on it. And Maggie gave me the biggest muffin with my hot chocolate.

Hospitals smell. And everyone whispers, except for the nurses who talk more loudly and cheerfully than they should. Even though Daniel's ward had a big colourful wall mural and the kids had their own things hanging above the beds and on their bedside chests of drawers, it was still a hospital full of sick children.

When we walked in Daniel and the Counsellor were leaning over a model of something.

'Oh Rain,' the Counsellor said, 'how lovely of you!'

'This is my dad, Brian,' I said, 'and his girlfriend, Julia. Hi, Daniel.'

The Counsellor looked tired but Daniel looked pretty much the same as usual. Diana said she might take the opportunity to slip out for a while, make some phone calls and buy some fruit, if that was okay with us.

'She's here all the time,' Daniel said.

'What are you making?' Julia asked. 'That looks like — it is! It's a model of the *Enterprise.*'

'Mum got it for me,' Daniel said. 'I'm into *Star Trek.*'

'So am I,' Julia said, and held up her hand in the Vulcan salute. 'Live Long and Prosper. What's your favourite, *Next Gen* or *Deep Space Nine?*'

After that, we all relaxed and the visiting hour flew

by. I kept sneaking looks at Julia, wondering how anyone with such perfect fingernails and hair could be a secret Trekkie, but she wasn't faking. I remembered Dad saying how he knew someone with every *Star Trek* video and I wondered why I hadn't worked it out then, that he had meant Julia. After all, Dad didn't know all that many people. It had to be her. I had just been too angry with him to really listen.

'What a great kid,' she said when we got in the car to go home again. 'I do hope he romps through that surgery and makes a full recovery. So intelligent! You are lucky to have a friend like that, Rain.'

She insisted that Dad drive to Minotaur Bookshop where she bought three *Star Trek* lapel pins, one for her, one for Daniel and one for me. 'For good luck,' she said. 'You can tell Daniel I'll wear mine and think of him every time I see it.'

I stuck mine through the band of my hat so I wouldn't lose it in the wash, and put Daniel's away so I could send it with the 'get well' card our class was making.

Or should have been, except that all our time was taken up with listening to and admiring Becky and Tom's American cousin, Madison, who was now over her jet lag. She was tall with bouncy hair and a perfect smile. And Becky was right, she had an opinion on everything.

'You're so cute, Rain,' she said, when Becky introduced me. 'In the States we'd say you were a real individual, the way you dress.'

I had on my blue wig, the one I'd bought at the Royal Show. It was hot and scratched the back of my head but I didn't care. All the other girls were pulling their hair back like Madison's, into pony tails that flipped at their shoulders.

'Well thanks, Madison.'

'And your name, too. Fancy naming anyone after the weather.'

'It's a poem, Madison. I'm named after a poem.'

'Whatever.'

When she saw my hat, though, she shrieked, 'Are you a Trekker?'

'Live Long and Prosper,' I muttered, doing the strange v salute I'd been practising.

'Oh girl, you should have told me! The one thing I'm just sick about is that I'm missing *Enterprise*, the new series. Back home everyone's watching it. Scott Bakula is a total stud puppy.'

I didn't have a clue what she was talking about, but I was interested to note that she now considered me her girlfriend. That's what she said when she hopped into Becky's mother's car at the end of school: 'Bye, girlfriend.' Becky was right, she was so American.

'I think Americans are actually aliens,' I told Maggie when I got home. 'I think they've been beamed up from somewhere really strange and far away.'

'You're probably right,' Maggie said. She was kneading bread dough in time to one of her celtic folk CDs. Every time the Irish hand drum banged, Maggie thumped the bread. It was soothing.

'Any news?' I asked.

'Diana has taken Daniel down to Rosebud for a few days,' Maggie said. 'They're waiting for his cardiologist to come back from that conference. And your father sent this up, special delivery.'

There was a computer sitting on Maggie's corner desk.

'Dad sent it?'

'Well, apparently it was chucked out at Julia's work. She scavenged it. Surprised?'

I nodded.

'It all works,' Maggie said, 'and I got us on the Internet straightaway so you can email Daniel anytime you want — they've got their notebook with them.'

I emailed Daniel before dinner about Madison and the new *Star Trek* series, *Enterprise*. And just after dinner I checked the email and found a reply from him. Reading it I could hear him talking and I missed him so much I got a pain under my ribs. I told Maggie and she said I shouldn't have had two helpings of butterscotch self-saucing pudding, but then she hugged me so my pain hurt worse.

'I know what you mean,' she said. 'I know just what you mean.'

I emailed Emma in Sydney, too, to give her our email address. I had only had a short note from her talking about the boys in her new school and how she didn't know which one to go out with. As if her parents would let her go out with anyone! Still, I guess I'd fibbed to her, too, about Daniel. Maggie emailed Fran and then we surfed the Internet for a while. Maggie checked out yoga sites and I looked for kids chat rooms, but the problem was that it just went on and on. As soon as you found one good place, there were a dozen links to follow. My head was spinning when I went to bed.

At school everyone talked about the disco and what they were going to wear. There was a rumour that the first prize for best costume was the new Circus Ponies' CD and everyone wanted to win it.

Becky and Madison were going as *Lord of the Rings* characters.

'Have you read the book?' I asked, surprised. *Lord of the Rings* was a big book and I couldn't somehow see Madison reading it.

'I've seen the movie. It was, like, awesome.'

'I've read the book,' Becky said, 'or at least part of it. Mum's making us these great long dresses. What are you going to wear?'

I couldn't make up my mind. Fancy dress was difficult. I wanted to be beautiful and glamorous. I wanted to be wild. I wanted to be mysterious and spooky. I didn't want to be anything from Harry Potter. I didn't want to be anything Halloweeny. I knew half the kids were recycling their Halloween costumes but I couldn't see the point.

'You'll have to make up your mind,' Maggie said, 'you're running out of time. But make it easy, will you, Rain? I'm going to start on that downstairs room tomorrow and I don't want to break off and make a complicated costume for you in the middle of sanding the floor. Can't you go as Alice in Wonderland, or maybe — hey, I've got it. Go retro — go as Dorothy, you know, from *The Wizard of Oz*.'

'Maggie, puhlease! That is like, so yesterday!'

In the end I emailed Daniel and asked his opinion and got an email back from Diana: 'Rain, I was making Daniel a costume. If you want to, you're welcome to wear it. Ask Maggie — she's got a spare key. It's in the sewing room hanging up under a plastic coat cover. Do wear it, Rain — it would make us all feel so good to know it was being worn.'

This was followed by an email from Daniel: 'Rain, I was going as Data but you could use the costume to go as Tasha Yar. Go to the video shop and see if you can get the episode, '*The Next Generation: Encounter at Farpoint*'. You'll see them both. Data's great — an android but he loves humans. He quotes, and writes poetry. But Tasha Yar is a girl. She got killed though. Your choice. I don't mind.'

Maggie and I went next door. It was weird going in when they were all somewhere else.

In the sewing room, just as the Counsellor had promised, was Data's suit. It was a top and pants in black with a mustard kind of inset in the top and the *Star Trek* badge, of course. It should have been a jumpsuit, but Diana had made the two pieces separate so you could more easily go to the toilet.

I thought it would be too small for me, but it fitted perfectly. I could see what everyone meant about Daniel having a growth spurt. I'd been taller than him when we first got to Clarkson and now it seemed we were the same height. The costume looked good. It looked like a proper costume, the sort you hire, not make yourself.

'Cool,' I said. 'It's really cool, isn't it, Mum?'

'It's fantastic,' Maggie said. 'Like it's so tomorrow! I really must do more than curtains with my sewing machine.'

We looked up Tasha Yar and Data on the Internet. Tasha Yar was a devoted Starfleet officer and a strong warrior. She was also quite beautiful. Data was an android with yellow eyes and pale skin. He knew everything but couldn't feel any emotions. Of course, I wanted to be Tasha Yar but I knew Daniel would have gone as Data.

'I haven't got yellow eyes,' I told Maggie.

'No, that's true. We could do the pale skin though,

with face paint. Look, it's a pity we didn't make a Seven of Nine silver catsuit for you. Look at the face paint she's wearing! Next fancy dress party, hey? Maybe your birthday?"

'Would you?'

'It wouldn't be a catsuit,' Maggie said. 'We'd do it the way Diana did, as two separate pieces. I don't see why not, Rain, if you want. Although by then you might want a different costume. Now, who is it to be — Data or Tasha Yar.'

'Data,' I said. 'I'll email Daniel. He'll give me all the facts.'

Daniel's surgery was scheduled for the day after the disco. I knew it wouldn't really make any difference who I went as, but it seemed important to have as many things piled up on Daniel's side as possible.

'You know,' Maggie said, the day before the disco, 'if we wanted to, we could give this costume a dress rehearsal.'

'What?'

'Well,' Maggie said, 'it would be possible for you to get dressed up after school as Data, and then we could drive down to Melbourne to the Royal Children's and show you in all your android glory to Captain Daniel. What do you reckon?'

I thought about it. I thought about walking in those huge hospital doors dressed as Data and I cringed. And then I thought of Daniel's ward, the beeping heart monitors and the pale kids, some of them only toddlers, and how hospitals always look like hospitals no matter how many wall murals there are, or mobiles.

'Okay,' I said.

I did look just like Data except that my hair was lighter and Maggie had had to tie it up in a little pony tail at the back.

When I walked into the ward Daniel gave me the biggest smile I'd ever seen. He looked fine, hardly even pale. I almost thought we'd got it wrong, that he didn't need surgery at all and they'd be sending him home.

When the visiting hour was over, Diana walked us out to the lifts, just as she used to walk us to the front door of our house.

'I hope everything goes well,' Maggie said, giving her a hug. 'You know if there's anything at all —'

'Thanks for what you have done,' Diana said. 'And Rain, thank you, too. Your emails have meant everything to Daniel, connecting him with the other world, with home.'

'I'm sure he'll be fine,' I said and allowed her to hug me, too.

Maggie and I walked back to the carpark in silence.

'I wish there was more we could do,' Maggie said. 'I feel powerless, you know?'

'You could make soup,' I said, 'for when they come

back. You could make your famous roast pumpkin soup, huge vats of it, and freeze it. Diana was going to make soup for us, you know, when we moved in.'

'Oh Rain, what a fantastic idea! Yes, I'll do that. Pumpkin soup and some celery soup and —'

'Maybe not just soup,' I said quickly before she got carried away. 'Maybe some casseroles or something.'

'I'll check with my yoga teacher,' Maggie said. 'Strength-building healing things, that's what they'll all need.'

The school disco was a huge success. Madison's eyes popped out when she saw me dressed as Data. Mind you, she looked pretty cool herself. Becky's mum had made her and Becky matching Elven princess dresses, with long drooping sleeves. They weren't good to dance in, though, and Madison fell over doing the Nutbush dance and the hems trailed in someone's spilled drink. I was pleased I had gone as Data, even though I didn't win the most original costume prize. That went to a little Year Two girl dressed as a dragon.

'You should have got that,' Becky said, looking a bit hot and flustered in her long medieval robes. 'You look so fabulous. I wish I'd thought of someone who wore pants. This skirt's giving me the creeps.'

'Skirts are so like, yesterday,' I whispered. I didn't want to hurt Madison's feelings. She couldn't help it if she spoke American. Becky and I cracked up. But even with all the dancing and the smoke machine and having our hair spray-painted, I couldn't help thinking about Daniel lying in his narrow hospital bed, waiting.

Maggie and I tried to pretend it was a normal Saturday the next morning. We did our chores but we didn't leave the kitchen in case the phone rang and we were both watching the clock, counting the minutes.

'Couldn't we ring?' I begged. 'Couldn't we ring the Intensive Care Unit and then we'd know?'

'He might not even be out yet,' Maggie said. 'We don't know how long the operation will take and we don't want to be bugging the busy staff. No, we'll wait for Diana to ring us, as we said we would, Rain.'

When the phone finally rang Maggie and I both stared at it, unable to move.

'Go on, Mum,' I said on the fourth ring, 'or she'll think we're not here.'

'Hello.' Maggie's voice sounded wavery and then there was silence and then she gave me the thumbs-up. 'Oh Diana, we're both so relieved. That's such good news. Thank god.'

We emailed everyone, of course, even Julia, who had actually visited Daniel in her own time and taken him some Star Trek novels.

'You won't be able to visit,' Maggie cautioned. 'He'll be in ICU for a few days. Then they'll transfer him back to the ward, and then after a week or so there he'll be home again. Children recover amazingly quickly.'

On Monday, Madison sat down with me and talked Star Trek the whole lunch hour, as if the costume had made me an instant soul mate.

'You are the most interesting person I've met in Australia,' she said. 'I just know we're going to be friends forever.'

When I got home from school there was a package on the kitchen table.

'For you,' Maggie said. She was at the stove stirring. She was taking the soup very seriously.

The package was small and addressed to:

Rain May and Captain Daniel
c/- 7 Cosmo Road
Clarkson

I turned it over. On the back it simply said: from Ensign Julia.

I opened up the packet and a little CD box fell out. Inside were two CDs neatly labelled '*Enterprise*, Episode One' and '*Enterprise*, Episode Two'.

'What?'

'There's a card,' Maggie said over my shoulder.

On the front of the card was a picture of a spaceship. Inside was the message:

Rain May and Captain Daniel,

Forwarding to you both the first episodes of the brand new *Star Trek* series. Hot off the optic fibre. More where they come from, same computer, same channel, next fortnight. Ask no questions, just download and enjoy.

'Do you know what she's talking about?' Maggie asked.

'No. But I guess we'd better put one in and see. It's a Star Trek thing, that's obvious.'

We put the CD in the CD drive of the computer. A boy came on the screen painting a model.

'It's a movie,' Maggie said. 'She's sent you a movie?'

The images were clear but jerky. It was like watching something that sometimes almost slowed down and then went back to normal speed. After the boy there was a field of some sort and an alien running through it pursued by some other aliens. He ran into this wheat silo and these little guys flattened themselves and went under the door of it. And then the silo exploded and a farmer came out and shot the alien. It didn't make any sense.

Then there was this stupid music and some credits started to come up and I realised that Ensign Julia had sent me pure gold.

'It's the latest *Star Trek* series,' I said to Maggie. 'It hasn't been released here yet. Wow! This is amazing. Daniel will be over the moon.'

'Will we watch it, or will we wait for Daniel?' Maggie asked.

'We'll watch this episode,' I said, 'so I can tell him about it. But we'll keep the other one until he comes home. Don't you think?'

'Okay.'

It was wonderful. It was exciting and even scary. I didn't like the flat guys one little bit but I loved the Doctor and his weird clown smile. And I thought the Chief Engineer was pretty cute.

'Madison will be so jealous,' I said at the end. 'This is the one thing she wanted to stay in the States for.'

'That?'

'Oh Maggie, you don't understand. She's a Trekkie. And she thinks Scott Bakula is a total stud puppy.'

'A what?'

'I prefer the Chief Engineer myself,' I said.

'Which one was Scott Bakula?'

'He's the Captain, Mum. Maybe you're just too old for this.'

I couldn't wait to tell Madison. I biked around to Becky's place straightaway. They were both in the bedroom.

'Have I got something to tell you,' I said.

'Hey girlfriend!' Madison said, putting her magazine down.

'I've just seen the first episode of *Enterprise*.'

'You've what?' Becky said, waving her fingers in the air to dry the polish.

'Where?' Madison asked. 'How?'

I ignored the questions.

'The music is so stupid,' I said. 'It completely stinks. But Chief Engineer Tripp is a total stud puppy.'

'Oh, how did you get to see that?' Madison said. 'I'd die for it. I would.'

'Ask no questions,' I said. 'Let's just say it was hot off the optic fibre.'

I told Madison a little more, about the Captain's dog and the way the Doctor said 'Optimism, Captain', just to get her going. And then Becky's mum came in and said it was nearly dinner time and I left.

'Oh Rain,' Madison wailed, walking me out to my bike, 'I've got to see it. You know I've got to see it. Is there any way I can?'

'I'll work on it,' I promised. 'I'll work on it for you, Madison, because after all we're girlfriends, right?'

'Power,' I said to Maggie when I got home, 'there's nothing like it.'

'Rain, I don't like that sentiment much,' Maggie said. 'Power is very, well, powerful, I guess. But you have to use it for good, not evil.'

'Oh, this is good power,' I told her. 'This is excellent power.'

The Captain's Log, Supplemental, Stardate 021101

Finally moved to Ward Seven West. A physiotherapist comes and makes me cough.

I've made a friend. There's an Indian boy in the bed next to me. His name is D'nesh Singh and he's from Fiji. He couldn't eat the food. He cried in the night because he couldn't eat the food and his father didn't know what to do, but then the Counsellor suggested he bring in some takeaway curry. Every night the curry smell in our ward threatens to overpower the hospital smell and the doctors and registrars come by and rub their bellies.

D'nesh's father is a doctor, too, and he also plays chess, so the Counsellor went out and bought a chess set for us. So far, D'nesh has won eight games and I've won nine. He coughs louder, though, and his scar is bigger.

If we're playing chess when the doctors make their rounds, sometimes one will peer at the game and suggest a move. I don't want to go back to school. I don't want to go back to school at all.

I tried to talk the Counsellor into letting me have the rest of the year off. I told her I'd study by myself. We could do it together. It'd be just as good, I said, as going back to school. Probably better. I'd learn more.

She smiled sadly at me. I think she'd secretly like me

to be at home. But my social skills would suffer, she and the Doctor agreed.

The only person I miss from school is Rain. She was so cool coming in as Data. That was amazing.

The thing is that she's drifting over to the girls' side. When she talks about school she talks about Becky and this American girl, Madison. She doesn't notice but she mentions them all the time now. So when I get back it'll just be me again. And I don't want it to be like that.

I wish I could go to Fiji with D'nesh. He says that in his school everyone respects you if you're clever. He said I'd be so popular at his school. He said I'd have the status of a warrior. Wow!

Trekkies Rule!

Madison was waiting for me at the school gate the next day.

'When can I see it,' she asked, 'when?'

'Well, the thing is,' I said, 'it's not mine. It belongs to a friend of mine.'

I'd thought about *Enterprise* and power and Daniel for most of the night. Honest, I'd hardly slept. I was so exhausted when Maggie called out that it was time to get up that I nearly faked a tummy ache to stay home, but I had to go to school because I had to put the plan in action.

Madison was wildly popular. Madison with her flippy pony tail and her weird way of talking was the girl everyone wanted to know and most of them wanted to be. She had it. Star quality. Don't ask me why. I couldn't understand it. Because she'd adopted me, the other girls, and even the boys, were including me in their games. Madison wouldn't play if Becky and I didn't play, so they had to.

I had something Madison wanted desperately. And I wanted something Madison had. I wanted to borrow some of her popularity. Not for me, I was doing fine. I needed it for Daniel. Because I could see that when he got back to school, it was all going to go back to being him sitting eating his lunch by himself, with me beside him watching the others play basketball.

'Who?' Madison demanded. 'Do I know them?'

'No, you don't. It's a boy called Daniel. He goes to school here, but he's in hospital at the moment. Becky and Tom know him, but they don't like him very much. Or at least, he doesn't think they do. So I don't think he'd like me lending the CD to you because you're their cousin.'

'But ... you could borrow it, couldn't you, and I could watch it at your place?'

'That would be cheating. Friends don't do that.'

'I've got to see it. I've just got to see it.'

'Well, one thing I thought of,' I said slowly, 'but it probably wouldn't work.'

'Yeah, yeah?'

'See, I thought we could start a *Star Trek* Club at school, a fan club. I mean there might only be the three of us, you, me and Daniel, but that would be okay. Then maybe we could persuade Daniel to let us meet sometime after school, at his house, and because we were in the club, he'd have to share. There'll be more episodes. We've, I mean, he's got two already.'

Madison practically swooned.

'I'll tell you what, Rain,' she said when she recovered, 'why don't we make this Daniel the president of the Club.'

'Brilliant,' I said. 'You've got to hand it to you Americans, you're fantastic at international relations.'

'Rain, you're weird, but I just love you.'

Of course everyone wanted to be in the *Star Trek* Club. We all put in fifty cents to join and that went to getting out the early videos to initiate the non-Trekkies among us. Our first meeting was at my place. We elected the office bearers — Daniel for President, Madison as Social Secretary, Becky as Treasurer. I offered to write the club newsletter.

There were a few murmurs about Daniel being President, but to my amazement Tom told everyone to shut up.

'We are lucky enough to have a dedicated Trekkie who knows everything about Star Trek,' he said. 'After all, what do you know, Oliver Canning? Anyway, if you're not happy you don't have to stay.'

In the end the club had fifteen members. Maggie made bucketloads of popcorn and we settled down to watch *Star Trek: The Original Series* with Mr Spock and Captain Kirk. The only person missing was Daniel himself but he'd be back. And he'd be back as

President of the Clarkson Primary School *Star Trek* Club. Actually, Madison suggested we cut out the Primary School bit, to make it shorter.

'Power,' I said to Maggie when everyone straggled home, still calling out 'Live Long and Prosper' to each other.

'I'm proud of you, Rain May,' Maggie said. 'When are you going to see Daniel?'

'Ensign Julia and I are going to deliver his official invitation to be President of the Clarkson *Star Trek* Club and to inform him that his first act should be the screening of *Enterprise, Episode One* accompanied by the Counsellor's killer chocolate cake. Julia's picking me up instead of Dad. Is that okay, Mum?'

'Yes, of course it is.' Mum put her hands on my shoulders and held me in front of her. 'It hasn't been too bad, has it, coming here to live?'

'It's been great, Mum. I'm sorry I was so horrid to start with.'

'And we pick up the puppy in a couple of days, Daniel comes home, Christmas is just around the corner.'

'Yep, looking good.'

'I want to know if it's okay with you if we all do Christmas together — Diana and Mark and Daniel and you and me. And you'd spend Christmas Eve with your dad and Julia.'

'It sounds great. I'd love that. Daniel will love that.'

'And Rain, I want you to know that I am so proud of you. You're the best. You know that?'

I wriggled away from her before she had a chance to get all kissy and weepy. I had things to do. I had an invitation to write.

The Captain's Log, Supplemental, Stardate 021101

I can't believe it. I just can't believe it. President of the Clarkson *Star Trek* Club. Elected President. They *all* elected me.

I was scared I'd cry in front of Rain but I didn't. I just sat there, my mouth wide open, until the Counsellor told me gently that I'd catch flies if I stayed like that any longer.

Turns out the American girl's a Trekkie, too, but she says Trekker, because that's what they say over there. And Rain's going to do a newsletter and she says the Club is all anyone ever talks about these days at school and everyone's waiting for me to come back because they all want to learn Volcan three-dimensional chess and how to swear in Klingon.

I know boys are not meant to say things like this. And I don't mean it in the way that you write your names on the bus seat or anything like that, but I'm really, really pleased Rain moved next door and became my best friend. And I know we'll be friends forever now, because you don't just forget seeing a platypus with someone, do you? Or how that person showed you who you could be, if you tried. And they cared enough.

On Daniel'

smile
we are cele
every brillia
but most of
our much mi
star boy
now home ag
welcome bacl
best friend

On Daniel's Fridge
smile
we are celebrating
every brilliant thing
but most of all
our much missed
star boy
now home again
welcome back
best friend